THE BOX OF DELIGHTS

OTHER YEARLING BOOKS YOU WILL ENJOY:

THE SECRET GARDEN, *Frances Hodgson Burnett*
A LITTLE PRINCESS, *Frances Hodgson Burnett*
BALLET SHOES, *Noel Streatfeild*
DANCING SHOES, *Noel Streatfeild*
SKATING SHOES, *Noel Streatfeild*
THEATRE SHOES, *Noel Streatfeild*
MOVIE SHOES, *Noel Streatfeild*
TRAVELING SHOES, *Noel Streatfeild*
TENNIS SHOES, *Noel Streatfeild*
A WRINKLE IN TIME, *Madeleine L'Engle*

YEARLING BOOKS are designed especially to entertain and enlighten young people. Charles F. Reasoner, Professor Emeritus of Children's Literature and Reading, New York University, is consultant to this series.

For a complete listing of all Yearling titles, write to
Dell Publishing Co., Inc.,
Promotion Department,
P.O. Box 3000, Pine Book, N.J. 07058.

The Box of Delights

WHEN THE WOLVES WERE RUNNING

JOHN MASEFIELD

ABRIDGED BY PATRICIA CRAMPTON

ILLUSTRATED BY FAITH JAQUES

A YEARLING SPECIAL BOOK

Published by
Dell Publishing Co., Inc.
1 Dag Hammarskjold Plaza
New York, New York 10017

Yearling® TM 913705, Dell Publishing Co., Inc.

ISBN: 0-440-40853-9

Reprinted by arrangement with Macmillan Publishing Company

Printed in the United States of America
First Yearling printing—December 1984

CW

To my wife

CONTENTS

[vii]

CHAPTER ONE

KAY WAS coming home for the Christmas holidays after his first term at school. The train stopped at Musborough Station and an old man ringing a hand-bell went along the platform, crying, "Musborough Junction . . . Change for Tatchester and Newminster."

Kay knew that this was where he had to change trains and, climbing down onto the platform in the bitter cold, he stamped his feet to get warmth into them. The old man ringing the hand-bell cried, "All for Condicote and Tatchester . . . All for Yockwardine and Newminster go to number five platform by the subway."

As the other passengers set off towards the subway entrance, Kay put his fingers into his pocket for his ticket. It was not there.

He went back to the carriage.

"Stand back, master, please," a porter said. "We're going to shift the train."

"Please, I think I've dropped my ticket in the carriage."

"Oh . . . one minute then," the porter said, opening the door. "Which seat were you sitting at?"

"Here," Kay said. He looked under the seat and in what he called 'the crink' between the back and the seat: there was no ticket there.

"I don't seem to see it," the porter said. "You'd better explain at the subway. We've got to shunt this train."

The train presently moved away and, returning to the bench where he had left his bag, Kay began to rummage through all his pockets.

An Irish terrier came up, sniffed at him and wagged the stump of his tail. "Good boy," Kay said, "nice old boy, then," and rumpled his head for him, which made the dog bounce about with delight. Still, he could not find the ticket. Then he noticed that the owner of the dog, a little old man in a worn, grey overcoat, was standing near him.

Since leaving the train he had been at the platform end, securing a big case in a cover of green baize. This he now carried in his hand.

"Ah, young Master," the old man said. "I see that my Barney Dog has made friends with you at first sight. That's the time that likings are made. And you're looking for your ticket, which, lo, is on the platform, dropped at your feet."

"Why, so it is," Kay said, picking it up. "So it is. Thank you ever so much."

"You must have slipped it out as you rumpaged," the man said.

Kay noticed that he had very bright eyes, alert as a bird's or squirrel's.

"We must be moving along, young Master," he said, "or they'll be wondering if we've got no tickets."

[2]

"Could I give you a hand, please, to help you carry your case?" Kay asked. He noticed that it was an awkward load for a little old man.

"No, I thank you, Master," the old man said. "But if you would be so kind as to steady her when I swing her, then I could get her to my back which is where she rides a-triumph. Only I do date from pagan times and age makes joints to creak. Or doesn't it?"

"I should think it does," Kay said.

"Now, I'm going to swing," the old man said, "and keep it, you, young Master, from rolling me over, if you will be so gracious." He swung his bundle up to his shoulder and indeed if Kay had not been there to steady it, the load might have overturned his frail little old withered body, 'like the ghost of ninepence,' as he said.

Kay walked with him through the subway to number five platform and there helped him to set down his bundle at a seat. The train came in, he got into a carriage and was soon on his way home.

When he had been taken to school in September he had gone by car. He was now returning home through a country quite new to him, by a railway line over which he had never before travelled. The train passed out of the meadows into a hilly land, beautiful with woodlands and glens. In spite of the bitter cold Kay was much interested in this new country. Some of the hills had old camps on them. On the headlands there were old castles; in the glens there were churches which looked like forts. Soon all the land to the left of the railway was a range of low wooded hills of the most strange shapes. He read the name on his cycling map – Chester Hills. "What a wonderful place," he said to himself. "I do wish that I could come here to explore." The train drew up at a station. "Hope-under-Chesters," he read. "Then that is Chesters camp."

He stared at the hills. It was a grim winter morning, threatening a gale. Something in the light, with its hard,

[3]

sinister clearness gave mystery and dread to those hills.

"They look just the sort of hills," Kay said to himself, "where you might come upon a Dark Tower and blow a horn at the gate for something to happen."

The train was about to start when, with cries of "Hold on!", two men, both in the black clothes of theological students, rushed across the platform and scrambled into the further corner seats of Kay's carriage. Both were youngish men (about twenty-three, Kay thought). Somehow, he didn't like the men, nor their voices. They made in some foreign tongue one or two remarks, which Kay judged to be about himself. After this, as the train went on, they spoke to him. One of them, a pale eager-looking man with foxy hair, said, "Going home for the holidays, ha-ha, what?" And when Kay said, "Yes, sir," the other said, "And very seasonable weather, too. We are to have snow, it seems. And no doubt you enjoy snowballing and tobogganing and making snowmen?"

Kay said that he did. He began to like this other man, who had a round, rosy, chubby face with fair hair; and yet there was something about him . . . Kay couldn't quite put it into words . . . he had a kind of a . . . sort of a . . . it was more in his eyes than anything else.

"I wonder," the chubby man said, "I wonder if, in the Christmas holidays, you will ever do card-tricks?"

"I don't know any."

"I wonder if I might try to teach you a simple trick," said the foxy-faced man, "since we are to be fellow-travellers."

Kay said that it would be very kind but he was afraid that he would be stupid at it.

"I see that you would be very clever at it," the foxy man said. "Don't you think, Tristan, that he has the face of one certain to be clever at card-tricks, what?"

"The very face," the other said.

"Just the facial angle and the Borromean Index," the foxy one went on.

"Let nothing tempt you into playing cards with strangers in a train or ship anywhere," the chubby man said.

"I'm inclined to agree with you, Lancelot," the foxy man said, "but there will be no harm in showing him one of the tricks by which sharpers deceive the unwary. Let me show you the commonest trick. It is often known as 'Spotting the Lady'."

He dealt out three cards, one of which was the Queen of Clubs, the other two low hearts. "See there," he said. "Mark them well. I twist them and shift them and lo, now, which is the Lady?"

"That one," Kay said.

"So it is, so it is," the man said. "What it is to have young eyes, Gawaine, is it not? And here is your sixpence. Now may we try once again? You're too young, you are too sharp, there is no getting round you. Now, no denial, if I beat you this time you shall give me half-a-crown for the Poor Box or next Sunday's collection."

Kay was about to protest, for he had promised never to bet, nor to play cards for money, but the chubby-faced man said, "Of course . . . that would be simply sportsman's honour."

"Agreed, agreed, what," the foxy-faced man said, as he twiddled the cards. "Now, which is the Lady?"

"This one," Kay said. "I saw her from underneath as the cards went down."

He was quite certain that he had seen the Queen, but when he lifted the card it was not the Queen, it was the three of Hearts.

"Now how did that happen, what?" the foxy-faced man said. "That will be just half-a-crown, please, for the collection in aid of the Decayed Cellarers, poor fellows."

Kay felt very unhappy, but pulled out his purse and paid the half-crown. It may have been suspicion or error, yet it seemed to him that both men were very inquisitive, craning over to see what money was in his purse.

Some slight noise made them all look towards the corridor. It was only the Irish terrier, Barney Dog, standing on his hind legs to look into the compartment. With a scratching of claws upon the paint, the dog dropped from his post and slid away. Yet Kay felt somehow uneasy, for the dog had looked at him so strangely.

"A dog, I think," the chubby man said, with a warning glance at his friend. "One of the friends of man, as they are called. And do you keep dogs at Seekings, Mr Harker?"

Kay jumped, for how did the man know his name and home? "How did you know about me, sir?" he asked.

"Magic, no doubt," the man said. "But there is a proverb:

> 'More know Tom Fool
> Than Tom Fool knows.'

Not that I want you to think that I think you a fool! By no means. And this is Condicote Station?"

There was always a press of people on Condicote platform at the coming-in of that train: there was on this day. Kay was bumped and thrust by people getting in and out. There was his guardian, Caroline Louisa, come to meet him.

When they had won through the press and were safely in the car, Kay found that he had been robbed.

"I say," he said, "there must have been pick-pockets in the crowd. They've got my purse and my dollar watch."

"Did you notice any suspicious person near you?"

"No . . . hullo, here's my ticket . . ."

"But you gave it up just now."

"So I did," he said. "Well. That's a queer thing. Why, there is the old man, that old fellow with the green baize case and the Irish terrier."

"What is he?" Caroline Louisa asked. "A Punch and Judy man?"

"I don't know," Kay said. "I'll ask him. And may I offer him a lift?"

[6]

"Ask him, if you like," she said. Kay got out of the car and went to the old man.

"Will you please tell me," he said, "if you are a Punch and Judy man?"

"I am, so to speak, a showman," the old man said, "and my Barney Dog is, as it were, my Toby dog when chance does call. But the secrets of my show, they aren't to be had by these common ones now, are they?"

"I was to ask you, would you like a lift down into the town as it is rather a step, and it is so cold."

"No, I thank you, my young Master," the old man said, "but now that the Wolves are Running, perhaps you would do something to stop their Bite? Or wouldn't you?"

"I don't know what you mean," Kay said, "but is there anything I can do for you?"

"Master Harker," he said, "there is something that no other soul can do for me but you alone. As you go down towards Seekings, if you would stop at Bob's shop, as it were to buy muffins now . . . near the door you will see a woman plaided from the cold, wearing a ring of a very strange shape, Master Harker, being like my ring here, of the longways cross of gold and garnets. And she has very bright eyes, Master Harker, as bright as mine, which is what few have. If you will step into Bob's shop to buy muffins now, saying nothing, not even to your good friend, and say to this Lady, 'The Wolves are Running', then she will know, and others will know, and none will get bit. But Time and Tide and Buttered Eggs wait for no man," he added. He swung away at once, bent under his pack, followed by his dog Barney.

Kay went back to the car.

"I'm sorry to have been so long," he said.

"About your being robbed," Caroline Louisa said. "Who was with you in the train?"

"Two men, but I don't think they would have robbed me. They were two sort of curates. They got in at Hope-under-

[7]

Chesters and got out here. The funny thing was that they knew my name and that I came from Seekings."

"They could have read that from your luggage labels," she said. "If your curates got in at Hope-under-Chesters they may have been members of the Missionaries' College there."

"I say," Kay said, "are there any muffins?"

"No," she said, "teacakes, but no muffins."

"Would you mind frightfully if we stopped at Bob's and got some muffins? Only you'll have to lend me some tin, for my purse is gone. I haven't a tosser to my kick."

"Now, Kay, you mustn't use slang in the holidays."

"By the way," Kay said, "are there Buttered Eggs for lunch?"

"Yes, specially for you. We must get on to them."

"You know," Kay said, "there's something very queer about that old man. He knew that there would be Buttered Eggs."

"Do you think he could have picked your pockets?"

"No, I don't. What do the curates do at Chesters?"

"They read good books and learn how to be clergymen and work in the farm and garden too, I believe. Did they want you to join them?"

"They didn't ask me. I wish you'd tell me about them."

"I don't know very much to tell. They're the other side of the county. I seem to have heard that most of them go off to Missions after a time of training. But I'm not telling you the news! I've got rather a shock to give you. All the Jones children are with us for the holidays."

"Oh I say, golly, whatever for?"

"The parents have to go abroad and I couldn't bear the children to have nowhere to go for Christmas. I do hope you won't mind frightfully."

"I don't mind at all," he said. "I like the Joneses . . . some of them. No, I like them all really. There's rather a gollop of them, though."

"I'm putting Peter into your room," she said.

[8]

"We'll have some larks, I expect," Kay said. "I do hope Maria has brought some pistols. She generally has one or two. Would you mind stopping at Bob's?"

She stopped the car in the busy market-place. Bob was the baker and confectioner of the little town. His shop was always sweet and pleasant with the smell of new bread. His window at this Christmas time was a sight to see, but Kay was not thinking of cakes or crackers. He looked only at the figure of a woman who stood near the shop window with her back to the wall. She was plaided over the head and shoulders with a grey plaid shawl.

Now, as Kay drew near, the woman, who had been motion-less, stirred. Her right hand came from underneath the plaid, drew it closer about her and held it there. Her hand was wearing what looked like a chamois leather glove. On the middle finger, outside the glove, very conspicuous, was a ring such as the old man had worn, a heavy gold ring arranged in a St. Andrew's Cross and set with garnets. At the same moment the woman shook the plaid back from her face so that Kay saw a pair of eyes so bright that they seemed to burn in her head. His heart beat as he said in a low voice, "The Wolves are Running." She looked hard at him, gave a very, very slight nod, and as Kay went on into the shop to buy the muffins, she slipped away sideways, walking very swiftly with an erect bearing. An old woman coming out of the shop with a basket shoved Kay aside, so that he lost sight of her.

When he had bought his muffins, he looked out with relish at the street, thinking how good it was to be home for the holidays.

Some Alsatian dogs were at the crossroads, testing the air with their noses, swaying their heads with the motion of a weaving horse, as though trying to catch a difficult scent. There were three or four of them. They padded about, casting this way and that, sometimes lifting, sometimes dropping their noses; somehow he did not like the look of them.

"I wonder who it is who has Alsatians?" he said to Caroline Louisa.

"Oh, a good many people have them," she said. "I never like them; they're too like wolves."

"Yes, they are like wolves, aren't they?" he said. "Are they the sort of dog that they have as police dogs?" But this Caroline Louisa did not know.

CHAPTER TWO

When they reached Seekings, there were the Joneses:
Jemima very smart, Maria very untidy, Susan like a little fairy,
and Peter, a good, honest sort of chap.

At lunch Kay said, "What asses we were not to ask that
Punch and Judy man to come here to give his show. Don't you
think we might go down and find him and ask him to come? Do
let's! We could have him in the study."

"Yes, certainly, you can have him if you can find him, and if
he will come."

"I do wish," Maria said, "that we could hear of a gang
of robbers in the neighbourhood come down to burgle
while people are at dinner, and hear all their plans, and
be ready waiting for them, and then have a battle with
revolvers."

"I hope we may get through Christmas without that," Caroline Louisa said.

"Christmas ought to be brought up to date," Maria said. "It ought to have gangsters and aeroplanes and a lot of automatic pistols."

After lunch, Kay went out to look for the Punch and Judy man. It was a dark, lowering afternoon, with a whine in the wind and little dry pellets of snow blowing horizontally. There was a kind of glare in the evil heaven, all the sky above the roofs was grim with menace and the darkness gave a strangeness to the firelight that glowed in many windows.

From the crossroads behind him a rider came cloppetting up, the horse slipping a little, the rider bent into a long white overall to keep the snow from blowing down his neck. "How do you do, Master Kay," the rider cried, checking his horse and looking down upon him. Kay did not recognise the man but he noticed that his eyes were very bright. The man suddenly put his right hand to his chin. The hand wore a pale washleather glove and outside the glove, on the middle finger, was a gold St. Andrew's cross, set with garnets.

"They tell me, Master Harker," the man said, "that Wolves are Running. If you see Someone," he added meaningly, "say Someone's safe."

"I will," Kay said.

"And look out for fun, Master Harker," the man said, shaking up the horse and riding on. Kay watched the horse go, skittering a little sideways and champing on the bit. It seemed to Kay that the man's arms were hung with little silver chains which jangled. Later it seemed to him that it was not a horse and rider at all, but a great stag from the forest. Certainly the figure that passed round the bend out of sight was a stag.

Kay went on to Lower Lock, which was a sort of double alley of very old houses near Tibbs Wharf, where the barges were lying up for Christmas. No matter at what time of the day or night you came near to Lower Lock, you would always meet a

[12]

dirty boy, doing nothing in particular. Kay used to enjoy going down to look at the barges and at the small sea-going vessels, colliers, top-sail schooners, brigantines and barquentines which sometimes came there. He saw the usual dirty boy as he drew near and recognised the lad as one called Poppyhead, which is the country name for ringworm. Poppyhead was sucking a straw under the lee of the bridge and beating his hands to try to warm them. On seeing Kay, he took the straw from his mouth and stared. "Please," Kay said, "do you know where the Punch and Judy show went?"

"What?"

"Do you know where the Punch and Judy show went?"

"Ah."

"Where did it go?"

"He's gone."

"He's not there," a woman who was passing said. "He's gone up to Cockfarthings in the Bear-Ward."

She was all wrapped against the snow in a grey plaid and Kay did not know who she was, but he saw a pair of very bright eyes and noticed a gold ring of odd shape on the hand that clutched the plaid close. She passed on over the bridge at once, without heeding Kay's word of thanks.

A very long time before, when the Abbot had ruled there, someone had kept bears for the amusement of the pilgrims coming to the Monastery and part of the village was still called the Bear-Ward, though perhaps no bears had been there for four centuries. Cockfarthings was the name of a man who kept a pub there called the Drop of Dew.

The only person in the bar was the little old bright-eyed man for whom Kay was looking. He sat in the settle by the fire looking at a book, which he closed and put in his pocket as Kay came in. Kay never quite knew why, but as soon as he saw the old man sitting there in the lonely bar he said, "If I saw Someone, I was to tell him that Someone is safe."

"Ah," the old man said, "but I say that that's more than

[13]

anyone knows when Wolves are Running, Master Harker."

"Please," Kay said, "will you tell me what you mean by Wolves?"

"If you keep looking out for fun," the old man said, "you will see the Wolves as like as not. Or won't you?"

"I don't know," Kay said.

"And now, Master Kay Harker," the old man replied, "you want me to go up to Seekings with my Punch and my Judy, and at half after five. I will be there. And perhaps," he added, tapping a little flat wooden box covered with some shining black cloth, "I'll bring more than my Punch and my Judy, for a travelling man collects as he goes, or doesn't he?"

"I should think he would," Kay said, not knowing what else to say.

"Ah," said the little old man, "you would think he would. And now, Master Harker, as I've heard tell that you're fond of birds, maybe you will tell me what bird you would like best to see, of all the birds there are."

"There is a bird," Kay said, "that I'd like frightfully to see, but I'm afraid it doesn't really exist."

"Ah, but perhaps it does exist, Master Harker," he replied. "Come, look now at the desert sands, where the pebbles are diamonds: look now, the spice tree; smell the spice upon it!"

As he spoke he pointed at the fire. The kettle on its hob was steaming a little but not enough to dim the glow in the grate. As Kay looked this seemed to open into a desert all glittering with jewels. Kay knew that it was an Arabian desert, for somehow Egypt with the Pyramids were behind him and mirages were forming far, far in the distance. Then, lo, in the midst of the desert was the sole Arabian tree, oozing gum, its leaves dropping crystals of spice, its flowers heavy with scent and its fruit shedding sweetness. Leaves, flowers and fruit all grew upon it at the same time.

As Kay looked, a wind parted the boughs and within, on a nest of cinnamon sticks, was a Phoenix.

"It's a Phoenix!" Kay said. "Now I can say I have seen one. Oh, I wonder, will it begin to sing?"

The Phoenix did begin to sing. She lifted her head and the plumes changed from white to gold and from gold to orange. As the song increased so as to shake the very house, the plumes changed from orange to scarlet and lo, they were no longer plumes but flames, which burned up the Phoenix so that the song died away and at last there was no Phoenix, nor any nest, only some ash blowing away in the wind and a few embers.

"Watch now," the old man said. Kay watched. Something stirred among the embers, something was being thrust from among them so that it fell with a little click upon the jewels at the tree-foot. Kay saw another thing fall, and then saw that these were fragments of egg-shell which the wind carried away.

Then out of the embers in the tree a little unfledged Phoenix rose, hopped onto a branch, pecked a flower, then pecked a fruit and crowed.

"There," the little old man said, "that is the bird you were afraid didn't exist. You shall see me at Seekings, Master Harker."

"Oh, but please," Kay said, "I was to settle with you how much we were to pay for the performance."

"I don't know that what you give me for my great show will be a fair pay for all the wonders seen," the old man said. "But five new silver shillings won't break you, that and a biscuit for my Toby and a dish of eggs and bacon afterwards for me."

Kay thanked him and went out from the Drop of Dew into the snow, which was now powdering the world and making all things dim. It was so bad that he thought it wise to take the short cut to Seekings, through Haunted Lane as it was called, which was a way he did not like, for it was a very dark lane of old houses. He was glad to get out of it into the open and so over the fence into the garden and into Seekings out of the snow.

When they had feasted on sausages, bread, butter, dripping and strawberry jam, the clock on the mantel struck for half-past

[15]

five. There came a noise of Pan pipes outside the window.

"Here is the Punch and Judy man," Kay said. "I'll fetch him in."

As he opened the door a whirl of snow sped in with the showman, bent under the frame of his show, looking rather like a giant without any head or arms.

"Do come in out of the snow," Kay said. The man came in and stamped the snow from him onto the mat, put down his show and brushed the sleeves of his coat.

"Wild weather, Master Harker," he said.

As soon as the room was ready and everybody comfortable on the floor, he came in and played his Punch and Judy play.

"And now, Master Harker and friends," he said, coming outside his stand, "I'll play more than my Punch and my Judy, for a travelling man collects as he goes."

He propped his theatre against a bookcase, sat cross-legged in front of the door and produced a little white ball, which he tossed into the air. It broke into two balls while it was aloft, he tossed them repeatedly until they broke into four balls, which shone as they flickered up and down. Presently, while three of the balls were in the air, he beat the fourth into the ground, where it became a little bright mouse which ran away into a hole. Then he tossed another ball to the ceiling where it became a shining bird which flew away; then he caught the remaining two balls, one in each hand. One turned into a red rose which he gave to Jemima, the other to a white rose which he gave to Susan.

"These are all little things," he said, "which a travelling man collects as he goes."

After this he turned to Maria, who was the smallest person there. "And you, Miss Maria," he said, "I am told you are fond of guns and that, so shall I see what will happen if I blow my bugle? But first I must tap the wainscot, to see if there's any gate there."

He walked across and tapped the wainscot, which was all

dark old wood with no hole or cranny in it, yet now after he had touched it, there was a tiny double gate of bronze, with gilded pinnacles, in the wood. As they all watched, the old man blew a little bugle and from within the wainscot a little bugle answered. Then suddenly a tiny voice called out an order and instantly two more tiny men pushed the double gates open and stood aside. A lot of little drums and fifes and trumpets struck up a march and out came a band of soldiers, headed by a drum-major. There must have been at least a hundred of them, with big drums as big as walnuts and little drums as little as filberts and tiny white ivory fifes and lovely little brass trumpets. Then after them came a regiment of foot-soldiers, then a regiment of cavalry on little horses. The band halted in the middle of the room but went on playing while the army marched about, three times round the room and then through the double bronze gates, which closed behind them. After they had closed the children heard the band fading away into the distance till it was silent. As they looked at the little gates they began to fade, till in a minute no trace of them was there; the wainscot was old, dark wood, in a solid panel.

"That was lovely," Maria said.

"Now," the old man said, "if you've been pleased with my shows, I'll be taking my way."

Kay paid him the silver shillings and brought in biscuits and some good meaty bones for Toby, and then a supper of eggs and bacon with hot-buttered toast, and a jug of sweet chocolate.

The old man seemed suspicious about the French window. Before he sat to his supper at the table he went to it to make sure that the curtains were drawn completely across it.

While he ate the children sat round the fire, talking of the wonderful show and telling each other what they would like to see again. Suddenly the dog Barney pricked his ears and from just outside the French window two key bugles and an oboe struck up the tune of 'O Come, all ye Faithful'. Some twenty singers outside in the snow broke into the hymn.

[17]

Peter went to the window and twitched back the curtains a little. "It's deep snow already," he said, peering out. "They've got Japanese lanterns. Do look how beautiful they are!"

Outside was a party of twenty men and women wrapped against the snow and bearing big Japanese lanterns hung upon sticks. Snow was whirling all about them and their faces glowed in the lantern light.

"That's the Cathedral choir from Tatchester," Caroline Louisa said. "There are the Canons and the Precentor, and that's the Bishop himself."

When the hymn had finished Kay and Caroline Louisa went into the hall to the side door. The Bishop and his singers moved towards them as they opened it.

"Good evening, Bishop," Caroline Louisa said. "Come into the warmth while we brew some cocoa for you."

Kay and the others brought buns and hot cocoa for the singers, who sat about in the hall eating and drinking.

"And now," the Bishop said, "I want you all to come tomorrow night to the Palace at Tatchester. We are having a children's party at five o'clock."

He looked about the faces gathered in the hall. "Ha," he said, "I think I have seen that face before. Aren't you my little friend, Miss Maria? Well, I am glad to see you again."

Little Miss Maria showed some small confusion, for once, only a year before, she had started the Bishop's motorcar and driven it into a lamp-post. However, the Bishop seemed inclined to forgive and forget.

A moment later he caught sight of the Punch and Judy man, who was packing his puppets into a box.

"And you're just the very man I was hoping to see," the Bishop said. "At this party tomorrow we shall have a great many children. Would you consent to play for them?"

"Right gladly," the old man said. "I will bring my Punch and my Judy and my dog Toby for I have played a Christmas play on that Night ever since pagan times, so to speak."

[18]

"Thank you," the Bishop said. "Then, another thing, I want you all to come on Christmas Eve to the Midnight Service of the Thousandth Christmas Celebration in Tatchester Cathedral. There has been a midnight celebration every Christmas Eve since the Foundation. We wish this Thousandth Festival to be really memorable."

As the members of the choir swathed themselves up against the snow Kay waited to open the door and heard, or thought he heard, the noise of swift, padding feet. The thought flashed into his mind that these were the Alsatian dogs again. 'They move just like wolves,' he thought.

He opened the door and saw three men trying to peer in through the French window. As the door opened they wheeled round and when the Precentor lifted his Japanese lantern as he left the house Kay saw that one of them was the foxy-faced man who had done the card-trick in the train.

"Aha, Precentor," he cried, "we were just too late for your concert, what?"

Kay noticed that Cole Hawlings came to the door as the last of the choir passed out. He leaned from it to watch the departing party and as he turned back into the house Kay thought that his face was very white.

The telephone bell in the porch began to ring and Caroline Louisa went to answer it. At the same moment Maria leaned over the banisters and cried, "Buck up, Kay! We're going to dress up and play pirates."

"All right. In a minute," Kay said.

He went back into the study to look after the old man, noticing that the curtains, which had been disarranged when Peter and the rest had stared at the carol-singers, were now carefully redrawn over the French window. The Punch and Judy man stood in the corner near the door, looking very white and tense, as though the earth were about to open.

"So, Master Harker," the old man said, "we always used to say 'It's the snow that brings the Wolves out'. Many a bitter

[19]

night did we stand the Wolf-guard, now here, once more, they're Running. We must stand to our spears."

"Everything's all right," Kay said.

"Where did those three men go?" the old man asked in a whisper.

"I think they went with the choir," Kay said, "but I couldn't see."

The old man shut his eyes and muttered something. It seemed to Kay that he was in great distress of mind. Then, as he opened his eyes, he smiled, pointed and whispered to Kay, "Master Harker, what is the picture yonder?"

"It is a drawing of a Swiss mountain," Kay said.

"And do I see a path on it?" the old man said.

As they stared at the picture it seemed to glow and to open. They heard the rush of the torrent and saw how tumbled and smashed the scarred pine trees were among the rolled boulders. On the lower slopes were wooden huts, pastures with cattle grazing and men and women working. Down the path came a string of mules in single file. Most of them carried packs upon their backs, but one of them, towards the end of the line, was a white mule, bearing a red saddle.

When it came to the turn of this white mule to round a corner, he swung out of the line and trotted into the room, so that Kay had to move out of the way.

"Steady there," the old man whispered to him, "and to you, Master Kay, my thanks. I wish you a most happy Christmas."

At that he swung himself on to the mule, picked up his theatre with one hand, gathered the reins with the other, said, "Come, Toby," and rode off out of the room, up the mountain pass, up, up, up, till the path was nothing more than a line in the faded painting that was so dark upon the wall. Kay watched him until he was gone and almost sobbed, "Oh, I do hope you'll escape the Wolves."

Caroline Louisa came into the study.

"I'm so sorry to upset your holiday. My brother is very ill

again and there is nobody to look after him. I'm afraid I must go up to him tonight."

"I say, I'm most awfully sorry," Kay said. "I'll see you off, it's such an awful night. I hope your train won't be snowed up."

"It's not so bad as that," she said. "Now I must run and get ready. I shall telephone you at ten tomorrow morning."

"You won't," Kay said. "All the wires will be down from the snow."

CHAPTER THREE

WHILE KAY was out of the house with Caroline Louisa the other children were in their rooms, dressing up as pirates and giving themselves pirates' moustaches with burned cork. Just as the front door slammed and the car lurched away to the station they came down to the study for a dress parade.

"Hold on a minute," Maria said, "I believe there's someone just outside that window."

"I expect it was only snow falling."

"No, somebody coughed – it's carol-singers again. Well, I'll tell them to sing and then we'll get on with Pirates."

"Let them ring the doorbell," Jemima said, "then somebody will attend to them."

"Not a bit," Maria said, "they're probably a lot of foul little boys trying to peep in at the window. I'm going to open this window to them here."

With that she flung back the curtain, unlocked the French window and opened it into the night. There, directly outside in the snow, was the figure of a man.

"Good evening, my young friends," he said in a gentle, silky voice. "I could not make anybody hear. This is the house called Seekings, is it not?"

"Did you want Caroline Louisa?" Jemima asked.

"I'm afraid you will think what I want is very absurd," he said. "I was given to understand that a man called Hawlings, a Punch and Judy showman, was here."

"There was a Punch and Judy showman," Maria said, "but he has gone."

"Gone?" the man said. "How long has he been gone?"

Although he had not been invited to come in out of the snow, he had come in and closed the French window behind him and was shaking the snow from himself onto the mat.

Maria answered in good faith, believing that what she said was true and little guessing what trouble her answer was to cause to others.

"He went away with the Tatchester choir," she said.

"And so, I miss him once more," he said.

"You would get him at Tatchester," Peter said. "The Bishop asked him to give a performance there tomorrow."

"Ah!" the man said. "So that fixes him to Tatchester." He looked at Peter curiously. "May I ask," he said, "if you are the gentleman known as young Mister Harker?"

"No," Peter said, "I don't know where he is at the moment. Probably upstairs somewhere, dressing up."

"Indeed!" the man said. "But I interrupt your Christmas gambols and if the man is gone I must go too." He slipped out, closing the French window behind him.

"Now, come on and play Pirates," said Peter. "Where on earth is Kay?"

At that moment Kay was driving home from the station. On his way through the market square he asked the driver to stop the car.

"You go home alone," he said. "I must do some Christmas shopping. I shall be back in a minute by the short cut."

With the money from Caroline Louisa he bought a little scissors case for Jemima and a sheath-knife for Peter, acid drops for Maria and a box of chocolates for Susan. Stuffing them into his pockets, he turned for home up the Haunted Lane. Near the most haunted part of the lane there was a short cut into Seekings garden across a derelict place known as Monk's Piece. No one much liked the place after dark, but Kay liked it better than Haunted Lane and in this night of snow it was a real short cut.

As he climbed the ruined wall into Monk's Piece he saw an electric torch flash in the main ruin. He had been told that the ghosts of monks gathered there at Christmas time, but ghosts of monks do not use electric torches.

Kay would have slipped past without pausing, but –

"So he was amongst the Bishop's choir and we never noticed, ha-ha, what?" said a familiar voice.

"Yes," a silky voice answered, and the silky voice was familiar to Kay, too. "And you never noticed. Do you notice anything, I sometimes wonder?"

Kay pressed close in to the ivy on the ruined wall.

"A clever dodge, though, what, to get in with the choir," the foxy-faced man said.

"No doubt it seems so to you," the silky voice replied. "I should have thought it the obvious dodge that you might have expected. Now he has got right through our ring again. Those fools let him trick them at Musborough. Then by sheer luck we got his message that he would be here and just as we learn his disguise and where he is, you let him go right through you with the goods on him. Oh, if I'd only not been tricked to the Drop of Dew for him I'd have been here and I'd have had him."

"You'd have thought him a carol-singer, just as we did," the other man growled.

"Would I?" the silky voice said. "Would I, my gentle Joe, my far-seeing friend? But come on now, the Wolves are Running. Get on to Tatchester." All the silkiness fell from the voice at a breath. The men jumped as though they'd been kicked, hurried out of the ruin, going away from Kay, and clumped along the Seekings garden fence. Presently he heard their car start off.

"So it's Abner Brown and his gang again," Kay muttered, thinking of past adventures. "I'm up against magic, then, as well as crime. And if anybody comes he's almost bound to see me. Oh dear, oh dear!"

Under the vaulted roof inside the ruin Abner stamped his feet and flogged with his arms. Kay had not waited a minute after the starting of the car before he heard a sort of scuttering, scraping noise coming from somewhere below. There were also little splashes and snarls. Someone was coming up by an underground way into the ruin where Abner was.

"Is that you, Rat?" Abner asked.

"Ah, it's me," a surly voice answered, "and what's the use of being me? Up in the attic and down in the cellar, all weathers, all hours, for one who'd sell his mother, if he had one, for what she'd fetch as old bones. And what do I get by it? Bacon fat, you might say, or the green of that cheese the dog won't eat, or the haggy that made the hens swoon. But I don't, my Christian friend, I get rheumatics; that, and the dog sicked at me. That's what."

"As a matter of fact, I've got some green-looking cheese for you," Abner said. "Look here."

There was the scratch of a match as Abner lit a candle-end. Kay found that he could see through a hole in the wall right into the ruin where, blinking at the light, stood a disreputable Rat he had known in the past but had not seen for years.

"Ah," Rat said, taking the cheese, which Kay could smell even in that cold weather. "And you wouldn't give me this if you could sell it to a Tourists' Rest."

"You're right," Abner said, "I wouldn't."

"I understand you, Abner, and you understand me," Rat said. He was eating the cheese with a sort of sideways wrench, while his little beady eyes stared at Abner.

"That man Joe, you'd better look out for, Abner," Rat said. "He's putting in for Chief, likewise the 'Ha-ha, what?' man."

"What d'you mean?" Abner asked.

"That's what," Rat said. Here he dropped his cheese on the floor, picked it up again and ate it without wiping it. "Ah, that's what," he repeated.

"What's your report?" Abner said.

"Him what you wot of," Rat said, "is a-getting rid of his Dog this evening."

"That's nothing," Abner said.

"A lady friend will take the Dog. That's what . . . Ah, and there's to be dark doings. You've scared 'em, Abner, and I beheld their scare."

"Well, this is news at last," Abner said. "What did you see?"

"They'd a meeting in the Lion and the Rose chamber at the Drop of Dew. One what you wot of will be trying to get out of your ring at dawn tomorrow, by Arthur's camp, across Bottler's Down, to Seven Barrows.'

"Will he have the goods on him?"

"Ah," Rat said, "that's what."

"Well, will he? And which of them is it?"

"I been a cellarman, I have," Rat said, "and I've gone marine cellarman. And I've been a poor man, living in the dark, though others live in the light with a haggy every day and grudge a poor man so much as a old fishbone, yes, they do. You says to me 'Find out what they decide'. Them was your words to me . . . 'Find out' . . . you says . . . 'what they decide'. There I've been in those dark dwellings in danger of Dog and found out what they decided. Now you says 'Will he?' and 'Which of them is it?' You didn't tell me about that."

"No, but you heard," Abner said.

"I found out what they decided," Rat said.

Abner seemed ready to box Rat's ears for his stupidity but he gulped down his wrath and said very sweetly:

"So you don't know?"

"I know what they decided," Rat said. "And why? Because I found it out. And how? By going the dark ways and being in danger of Dog. What your words was to me, that I done, although in danger of Dog."

"And you did well," Abner said. "My brave Rat, you did superbly."

"That's what," Rat said.

There was a pause. Abner said nothing, but Rat seemed to be expecting something. At last he said, "You said I was to have a bacon rind over and above my cheese."

"So you shall have, my brave Rat," Abner said, "I'll bring you one tomorrow."

"That's the bacon rind to bring the plump on a man," the Rat said, "bacon-rind-tomorrow. That and marrow-bone-the-day-after proper makes your fur shine. Is there any little dark job you want done then, Master Abner, or shall I go now?"

"I want you to report at eleven tomorrow at the usual place, in case there should be anything."

"That Kay Harker, what you wot of," Rat said. "If you was to saw his head off you'd do a good deed. He's to have a Dog give him at Christmas. That's what." He moved off into the underground passage singing a song to his one tune, 'Sally in Our Alley':

> "The nights are cold
> And on the wold
> The wintry winds do whist-ol.
> I ride my grey
> On the high way,
> To shoot 'em with my pist-ol".

Abner took a few paces to and fro within the ruin. Kay could hear some muttered words: "Well, the chances are that the Box will be on the man who tries to get out of the ring. Bottler's Down, eh? As nice a quiet place for a scrobbling as ever was made. We'll stop whoever it is. And, of course, it may be Cole, Box and all. It probably will be . . ."

So saying, he flashed a torch on the broken stones of the floor and walked briskly away, passing within two yards of Kay. When he had gone Kay slipped from his hiding-place and returned to Seekings.

"I say, Kay, wherever have you been?" Peter said. "We've been waiting simply ages for you and you aren't dressed or anything and we were just going to play Pirates and there has been a clergyman sort of chap here asking for the Punch and Judy man."

"What did you tell him?" Kay asked.

"Oh," Maria said, "I told him he had gone with the Tatchester choir."

'So that's how he thought that,' Kay thought to himself. "Well," he said aloud, "he has gone on to Tatchester, you say?"

"Yes," Peter said, "I told him that the Bishop had engaged him to play tomorrow."

"Come on then," Kay said, "let's play Pirates."

After they had played Pirates they had supper. Then presently it was time for all the children to go up to bed. Kay and Peter were the last to go up. They got into their beds and talked to each other across the room about what they would do in the holidays.

It was very snug in their room, for Ellen had built up the fire. Peter had just said that he thought he would be getting off to sleep when Kay was thoroughly startled by the whining cry of the wind in the chimney. Often on snowy nights he had heard that cry of the wind but tonight there was something in the shriek that was very awful.

[28]

"I say, Peter," he said, "did you hear that? It was just like wolves howling."

"Wolves are extinct," Peter muttered, half asleep. Kay was just on the brink of sleep when the wind again howled.

"It was wolves," Kay said. "It was what the old man said, 'The Wolves are Running'."

Kay could not have been long asleep when he woke up feeling certain that there was something important to be done at Arthur's Camp. He sat up in bed, struck a light and lit a candle. Peter woke up very grumpily. "What on earth are you lighting a candle for?" he said.

"I'm going out to Arthur's Camp," Kay said. "Will you come along? I feel that I'm wanted there."

"Wanted?" Peter said. "You're talking in your sleep. What time is it?"

"Nearly midnight," Kay said.

"Well, who on earth would want you there at midnight?" Peter growled.

Kay said, "I'll go alone." He wrapped himself up in thick things, slipped downstairs, pulled back the bolts and opened the front door. There outside was a shining white pony, with a proud Arab head and scarlet harness and headstall. "Mount and ride, Kay," the little horse said, "for the Wolves are Running."

Kay at once mounted and the horse sped over the garden with him, making no noise at all. Soon the houses dropped behind and there was the open country, looking very wild and strange under the snow. At last the horse turned off on the track to Arthur's Camp. At this moment Kay heard on the wind a note which he had heard once before that night. It was faint and far away, but it was the cry of Wolves Running.

All the trees were gone; it was now a bare hill with a kind of glare coming from the top of it. By this glare, Kay saw that the

[29]

earthen wall of the camp was topped with a wooden stockade, which the horse leaped.

By the light of the fire within the stockade Kay saw that the camp was busy with many short, squat, shag-haired men and women, among whom some wizened savage children darted or cowered. Penned in one place were some half-starved cows, in another place some long-legged sheep. Whoever these people were, they had certainly been roused in the midnight by an attack of some sort. Somewhere down on the hill-slopes, coming towards them, that cry which had so scared him now burst out with a frenzy of nearness which made Kay's blood run cold.

"The Wolves are Running," he muttered. "And now here they are."

Just three feet from him a big Wolf leaped to the stockade and almost scrambled to the top. A man struck at it with a kind of adze and the fierce head fell back, but with a worrying, yapping snarl the rest of the pack came over the palisade in a body behind Kay. The men shouted and ran at the Wolves. A woman thrust a great piece of gorse into the fire, lit it and ran with it blazing. Kay seized another bit of gorse and did the same and for the moment the glare was too much for the Wolves, which drew away without giving up the attack. Kay could see them not far away, sometimes as green eyes glaring, sometimes as darknesses in the snow. They were waiting for the fires to die down, getting their breath, laying their plans and licking their knocks and singes. Kay wondered how he was to get home to Seekings with the Wolves in the fields. "They always said there aren't any wolves," he muttered, "but there could easily be wolves in places like Chester Hills and now, in this wild winter, out they come."

The men now drove the stock to a space all lit and cornered by fire. Great flakes of fire floated away into the wind as the dead leaves took flame, blots of snow fell hissing among the embers. The cattle flinched at both.

[30]

Kay knew that wolves are creatures of extraordinary cunning. He noticed that the pack shifted away from the palisade, the cattle inside the enclosure became quieter, the men and women put out the flares they were burning and there was a general slackening of the attention. Then, suddenly, from the darkest point of the camp there came a howl and the noise of rushing bodies. The pack was over the stockade and into the camp, the cattle were stampeding and the people shouting and lighting flares again.

Kay said to himself, "This is the real attack. The others were only feints to find out how the land lay." Two enormous Wolves with red eyes and gleaming teeth rushed directly at him.

He left himself plucked by the arm. There was the old Punch and Judy man, now wearing a white stuff that shone.

"You come here beside me, Master Kay," he said. "Don't you bother about these things, you only see them because I'm here. But it's like old times for me to see this. I've had fine times on winter nights when the Wolves were after the stock. And the thing to do is to follow them, Master Kay, and never to let up until you've caught them, for the Wolves lose heart and they're not half what you'd think they'd be when you see them like this.

"But I hoped that you would come, because other Wolves are Running. They're running after me and they're running me very close. It's not me they want, it's my Box of Delights that you caught sight of at the inn. If I hand that to you, Master Kay, will you keep it for me so that they don't get it?"

"Of course," Kay said, "I'll keep anything for you that you want kept, but if you're in danger from anybody go to the magistrates, they'll defend you."

"Ah," he said, "the magistrates don't heed the kind of wolf that's after me. Now, there are three things that I must tell you about this little Box: you open it like this. If you push this to the right you can go small and if you press it to the left you can go swift. I've not had this long, it is Master Arnold's, not mine and though I've sought for him and called him, I have not found

[31]

nor been heard. He's gone a long way back, Master Arnold has.

"If I had time, Master Kay, I might best the Wolves, but they run me close with this New Magic which I can't guard myself against, not any more, for I'm old now and only know the Old Magic. So will you keep this for me until I'm able to claim it, if I ever may be able, or till old Master Arnold can come back for it?"

"If I possibly can, I will, of course. But who is this Master Arnold and how shall I know him?" Kay said.

"You'll know him if he comes," the old man answered, "for he'll come right out of the Old Time, but above all things keep it from coming to them. Now, one other thing. If you and your friend Master Peter would come out this way towards dawn, you may see what comes to me. And now, good fortune, Master Kay, and I hope that I'll come back for this Box of Delights before so very long and give it to Master Arnold in person." He handed Kay the little black shiny box. "Put it in your inner pocket," the old man said.

Kay was about to put it in his pocket when somebody thrust a big gorse bush into the fire. It flared up with a blaze and crackle. Instantly the cattle and the tribesmen had disappeared, leaving Kay alone in a glare of light, surrounded by a ring of Wolves all snarling at him and glaring with red eyes.

"Never heed them," the little old man's voice said from far away. "Press it to the left and go swift."

Kay pressed the catch to the left and in a flash he was plucked up into the air away from the Wolves and the hillside and there he was, rather out of breath, in his bed at Seekings, with Peter sitting up in the bed opposite saying, "I say, Kay, what are you doing? Haven't you gone yet? What's the time?"

"Quarter to one," Kay said.

"Uh," said Peter with a growl, rolling over.

CHAPTER FOUR

AT SIX o'clock Kay woke again and heard the bells chiming for the hour. What with the moonlight and the snow-blink, there was light enough for him to see the Box.

"He said I must go out towards the Camp at dawn with Peter," he muttered. "I say, Peter, wake up. Let's go and explore."

"Get up before light on the first day of the holidays – I think it's the purple pim!" Peter said.

"Oh, get up, Peter," Kay said. "We can forage in the larder and then have a real breakfast when we come in."

"Oh, all right," Peter said.

Before they set out they got themselves ham and bread which they spread with blobs of butter from the larder. Then each had a big mincepie and a long drink from a cream pan. When

[33]

Peter was outside, Kay looked at the little black Box in his inner pocket before stepping out into the white world of the snow and the road to Arthur's Camp.

At the camp the wood was again in its place, all bracken and brambles prone under the snow, no close cover left. There were no wolf-tracks in the snow under the ramparts where the wolves had run, but there were many rabbit-tracks.

Kay was soon at the very place where he had stood within the stockade when the fires had burned and the beasts had stampeded. In the space between three yew trees where the old man had spoken to him, someone had scuffled aside the snow. The strange thing was that no footprints led to the place, although footprints led away from it.

They followed the footprints, which were those of a man about the size of Cole Hawlings, over the camp wall, across the ditch and presently out of the wood onto the bleak upland known as Bottler's Down. As the boys came over one of the shoulders they sighted their quarry two hundred yards ahead, a little old man trudging the snow, bent under a green baize-covered bale, near a spinney called Rider's Wood.

At that instant four men darted out of Rider's Wood and ran at the old man, who dropped his bundle. A sack or bag came down over the old man's head and in the same instant rope was lashed round his arms and legs. In five seconds they had him trussed up and carried to the other side of the spinney. The boys stood spellbound, too startled to cry out or to do anything.

There came the roar of an engine from beyond Rider's Wood. "That's an aeroplane," Kay said. They heard confused noises and the slamming of a door. The roaring of the engine became much louder and an aeroplane lurched into sight, going across the snow to take off into the wind.

"It will stick in the snow," Kay said, "and then they'll have to leave him."

However, it didn't stick in the snow, it lifted after a short run and at once rose higher and higher, with great lolloping leaps.

Now that it was in the air it was silent, of a grey colour and swifter in going and climbing than any he had seen.

"They scrobbled the old man!" Peter said.

"Well, that's that," Kay said. "They've got him and they've got away with him and I'm pretty sure it was our Punch and Judy man."

"It looked jolly like him," Peter said. "Well, we'd better go back and tell the police."

The big red-faced Inspector was an old friend of Kay's who understood rabbits and was a clever amateur conjurer. Kay told his story, Peter backing him up.

"Ah, indeed," the Inspector said, "that was those young officers from the aerodrome having a bit of a frolic."

"It wasn't like a frolic," Kay said and Peter added, "And they weren't in uniform and it wasn't a government aeroplane."

"Besides," Kay said, "it was such a lonely place and such a time in the morning."

"And what were you doing in that lonely place at that time in the morning, Master Kay?" the Inspector said. "I hope you young gentlemen weren't trespassing in pursuit of game."

"No, of course we weren't. We were out looking at the tracks of animals in the snow."

"Ha!" the Inspector said. "Now, did this old man struggle at all or cry out?"

"He didn't have a chance to," Kay said.

"Did he see you or did the other people see you?"

"No, they couldn't," Kay said, "from where they were."

"And did you shout or try to raise an alarm?" the Inspector asked.

"I'm afraid we didn't," Kay said. "We were just spellbound. They ran out, scrobbled him up, put him into the aeroplane and away they went."

"Well," the Inspector said, "it sounds like the aerodrome to me – those young fellows, Master Kay, serving their country

[35]

and away from the civilising influence of their mothers, just full of spirits, the spit of what I was myself when I was a young man. It was a Christmas gambol and a bit of what you call ragging. And you see, Master Harker, the Law isn't like ordinary things. Sometimes the Law has to put its foot down, sometimes it has to shut its eyes. And the Law makes much of what is called 'motive', when what's prank when meant as prank may become felony when meant as felony. What you saw was no more than a prank.

"All the same, I am obliged to you, Master Harker. We in the Law are always glad of evidence from one who knows what's what, so I'll keep my eyes and ears open and I'll ask what aeroplanes were out that way this morning. You're sure you didn't recognise any of the parties?"

"Well," Kay said, "we both think the man was the Punch and Judy man who was at Seekings House last night."

At this moment the telephone bell rang. The Inspector lifted the receiver. "Yes," he said, "Condicote seven thousand. What is it?" Someone talked to him for a minute or two. "Now that," the Inspector said, "that's what we call in the Law a coincidence. That was our officer at Tatchester asking about your Punch and Judy man, Cole Hawlings. He's at Tatchester now and the Police are asking, 'Is he a fit kind of man to give a public performance at the Bishop's Palace this very night as ever is?' Now is he, Master Harker, a kind of man to perform before a Bishop?"

"He's simply wonderful," Kay said.

The Inspector spoke into the receiver again. "I have every reason to suppose," he said, "from information received, that the man is a good performer and can be trusted not to disappoint nor yet to shock the company. By the way, is the man there?"

He listened and then said, "Just bring him to the telephone. There's a young gentleman would like to know something. Hallo, Mr Hawlings? Are you any the worse for being in the aeroplane? He says, 'None the worse, sir.' Mr Hawlings, who was it put you in the aeroplane? He says, 'Some young friends, with more fun than sense.' And what brought you out Bottler's Down way in the snow, Mr Hawlings? He says, 'It was the only flat bit where he could meet the aeroplane.'

"Now here's a young friend wants to ask how you are."

The Inspector handed over the receiver to Kay.

"Is that you, Mr Hawlings?" Kay asked. "I rang you up to ask how you are . . . If you are any the worse for the Wolves or the aeroplane?"

The telephone was full of crackles and buzzes. A female voice said, "Pottington two five, please." A distant man's voice said, "Give up the strychnine and go on with the belladonna," then from far away an old man's voice said, "No, none the worse I thank you – all the better."

"You are really Mr Hawlings?" Kay asked. "That found my ticket and was scrobbled into the aeroplane?"

"Really, truly he," the voice answered. "Goodbye, my young Master." Kay hung up the receiver.

"So that's that," the Inspector said. "That's how Science helps the Law. You thought your friend was scrobbled. Now by Science and the Law you hear from his own lips that all is well."

Somehow Kay wondered if all was well. The telephone was working badly and the voice was like the old man's voice, but still, somehow he felt uneasy.

"I'm very glad," Kay said, "that the man is safe. Please forgive us for taking up so much of your time."

"A public man's time is the public's," the Inspector said. "It's my duty, as a public man, to listen to all and sundry at all times. Sometimes there isn't enough for the Law to go upon but any tale that's first-hand evidence, you bring it to the Law and depend upon it, Master Kay, murder will out. However dark the deed, we bloodhounds of the Law, as they call us, will bring it into the limelight."

[37]

Kay thanked him again, then after talking for a moment of brighter topics – rabbits, simple conjuring tricks, the Condicote rugby team, etc – they both shook hands with the Inspector and went home to breakfast, for which they were a little late.

As soon as he was in the house Kay tried to telephone Caroline Louisa to ask how her brother was, but the line was out of order owing to the snow. They said the men were doing their best but couldn't promise anything.

All through breakfast the snow fell from roofs and trees, slither, slither, splosh. When they went into the field to set about their snowman they found the snow rapidly becoming too slushy.

"We'd better stop," Jemima said. "We shall be wet through. He'll never look up to much."

"We'll give him a sort of head," Kay said. Maria topped it with an old top hat that had lost its crown, Susan put in some dark stones for the eyes and Peter added a clay pipe. Then they flung some sploshy snowballs at him.

Ellen called to them from the door: "If you please," she said, "you're not to get wet through."

"Oh, by the way, Ellen," Kay shouted, "have you had any telephone message?"

"No, the telephone isn't working," Ellen said.

"Are they doing their best?" Peter called.

"Oh, Miss Susan," Ellen said, "you are naughty to get yourself wet through like this, and you, Miss Jemima. Miss Maria, your things will be ruined."

"Jolly good job," Maria said.

"No, Miss Maria, it isn't a good job and you know that it isn't and you ought not to say such things. To be wet through in the cold is the way to take your Death. Come along in now, you must change all your things." She shepherded the girls to the door and then remembered the boys: "And you, Master Kay, you're wet through too," she said.

"Oh, come on, Peter," Kay said. "Let's get out of this. There's too much discipline here altogether."

They slipped over the fence in spite of Ellen's calls.

"Shall we go out again to Arthur's Camp?" said Kay.

"But you've been there once this morning."

"I know, but I don't think we've heard the last of that aeroplane . . ."

Like trackers on a trail, they went cautiously. When they came in sight of the spot where the old man had been set upon they saw two men sweeping the snow with a sort of hard handbrush.

"I see it all," said Kay. "They scrobbled the old man thinking that he'd got something they wanted and released him when they found he hadn't got it. Now they think he's dropped it in the snow and they're looking for it."

"They look like two curates to me," Peter said.

"They're the two who were in the train with me yesterday and I've a very shrewd suspicion that they picked my pockets."

"Golly!" Peter said. "You think the curates' clothes are a disguise? Well, let's watch."

Presently the two men wearied of their search and went off down the hill to the road where a big, shabby car was waiting for them. They got in and drove off in a north-westerly direction and presently, looking that way, he saw a bright, moving speck in the sky which he judged to be an aeroplane.

"I wonder what it was," Peter said. "I wonder what it was the men were hoping to find."

Kay knew very well what it was they were hoping to find, but he did not feel that he had a right to say. They went home.

Now at last, Kay felt that he was free to look at the Box of Delights. He went up to his bedroom, but even there he was not sure that he could guard himself from being seen. Remembering how those spies had been peering in at the window the night before and how the repulsive Rat had crept about in the secret passages finding out all sorts of things, he locked both doors and hung caps over the keyholes, looked under the beds and finally, as in the past when he had wished to hide from his governess Sylvia Pouncer, he crept under the valance of his dressing-table. No one could possibly see him there.

The Box was of some very hard wood of a very dense grain, covered with shagreen which was black with age and sometimes worn away to show the wood beneath. Both wood and shagreen had been polished until they were as smooth as polished metal. On the side there was a little counter-sunk groove in the midst of which was a knob in the shape of a tiny golden rosebud.

Kay pressed the knob and at once from within the Box there came a crying of birds. As he listened he heard the stockdove brooding, the cuckoo tolling, blackbirds, thrushes and nightingales singing. Then a far-away cock crowed thrice and the Box slowly opened. Inside he saw what he took to be a book, the leaves of which were all chased and worked with multitudinous figures, and the effect that it gave him was that of staring into an opening in a wood. It was lit from within and he saw that the tiny things that were shifting there were the petals of may-blossom from giant hawthorn trees covered with flowers. The hawthorns stood on each side of the entrance to the forest, which was dark from the great trees yet dappled with light. Now, as he looked into it, he saw deer glide with alert ears, then a fox, motionless at his earth, a rabbit moving to new pasture and nibbling at a dandelion and the snouts of the moles breaking the wet earth. All the forest was full of life, all the birds were singing, insects humming, dragonflies darting, butterflies wavering and settling. It was so clear that he could see the flies on the leaves brushing their heads and wings with their legs. "It's all alive and it's full of summer, there are all the birds singing, there's a linnet, a bullfinch, a robin, and that's a little wren." Others were singing too: different kinds of tits, the woodpecker drilling, the chiff-chaff repeating his name, the yellowhammer and garden-warbler, and overhead, as the bird went swiftly past, came the sad, laughing cry of the curlew. While he gazed into the heart of summer and listened to the murmur and the singing, he heard another noise like the tinkling of little bells.

"Where did I hear that noise before?" Kay said to himself. He remembered that strange rider who had passed him in the street the day before. That rider, who seemed to have little silver chains dangling from his wrists, had jingled so.

"Oh," Kay said as he looked, "there's someone wonderful coming."

At first he thought the figure was one of those giant red deer, long since extinct, with enormous antlers. Then he saw that it was a great man, antlered at the brow, dressed in deerskin and moving with the silent, slow grace of a stag, yet hung about with little silver chains and bells.

Kay knew at once that this was Herne the Hunter, of whom he had often heard. "Ha, Kay," Herne said, "are you coming into my wild wood?"

"Yes please, sir," Kay said. Herne stretched out his hand, Kay took it and there he was in the forest between the two hawthorn trees, with the petals of the may-blossom falling on him. All the may-blossoms that fell were talking to him and he was aware of what all the creatures of the forest were saying to each other, what the birds were singing and what it was that the flowers and trees were thinking. And he realised that the forest went on and on for ever and all of it was full of life beyond anything that he had ever imagined, for in the trees, on each leaf and every twig and in every inch of soil there were ants, grubs, worms, little tiny, moving things, incredibly small and yet all thrilling with life.

"Oh dear," Kay said, "I shall never know a hundredth part of all the things there are to know."

"You will, if you stay with me," Herne the Hunter said. "Would you like to be a stag with me in the wild wood?"

There was Kay in the green wood, beside a giant stag, so

screened with the boughs that they were a part of a dappled pattern of light and shade and the news of the wood came to him in scents upon the wind. They moved off out of the green wood into a rolling grassland where some fox-cubs were playing with a vixen, and presently came down to a pool where moorhens were cocking about in the water, under the fierce eye of a crested grebe. It was lovely, Kay thought, to feel the water cool upon the feet after running, 'and it's lovely too,' he thought, 'to have hard feet and not get sharp bits of twigs into one's soles.' They moved through the water towards some reeds where Kay saw a multitude of wild duck.

"Would you like to be a wild duck, Kay?" Herne asked.

At once, with a great clatter of feathers, the wild duck rose more and more and more, going high up, and, oh joy! Herne and Kay were with them, flying on wings of their own and Kay could just see that his neck was glinting green. There was the pool, blue as a piece of sky below them and the sky above brighter than he had ever seen it. They flew higher and higher in great sweeps and presently they saw the sea like the dark blue on a map.

"Now for the plunge!" Herne cried and instantly they were surging down swiftly and still more swiftly and the pool was rushing up at them and they all went skimming into it with a long, scuttering, rippling splash. And there they all were, paddling together, happy to be in water again.

"How beautiful the water is," Kay said. Indeed it was beautiful, clear hill-water, with little fish darting this way and that and the weeds waving.

"Would you like to be a fish, Kay?" Herne asked, and instantly Kay was a fish. He and Herne were there in the coolness and dimness, wavering as the water wavered and feeling a cold spring gurgling up just underneath them, tickling their tummies.

While Kay was enjoying the water Herne asked, "Did you see the Wolves in the wood?"

"No," Kay said.

"Well, they were there," Herne said, "that was why I moved. Did you see the hawks in the air?"

"No," Kay said.

"Well, they were there," Herne said, "and that was why I plunged. And do you see the pike in the weeds?"

"No," Kay said.

"He is there," Herne said. "Look!"

Looking ahead up the stream Kay saw a darkness of weeds wavering in the water and presently a part of the darkness wavered into a shape with eyes that gleamed and hooky teeth that showed. Kay saw that the eyes were fixed upon himself and suddenly the dark shadow leaped swiftly forward with a swirl of water. But Kay and Herne were out of the water. They were trotting happily together over the grass towards the forest, Herne a giant figure with the antlers of the red stag and himself a little figure with budding antlers. And so they trotted together to a great ruined oak tree, so old that all within was hollow, though the great shell still put forth twigs and leaves.

Somehow the figure of Herne became like the oak tree and merged into it till Kay could see nothing but the tree. What had been Herne's antlers were now a few old branches and what had seemed silver chains dangling from Herne's wrists were now the leaves rustling. The oak tree faded and grew smaller till it was a dark point in a sunny glade, and there was Kay standing between the two hawthorn trees which were shedding their blossoms upon him. These too shrank until they were as tiny as the works of a watch and then Kay was himself again under the valance in his room at Seekings, looking at the first page in the Book of Delights contained within the Box.

"No wonder the old man called it a Box of Delights," Kay said. "Now I wonder how long I was in that fairyland with Herne the Hunter?" He looked at his watch and found that it was ten minutes to eleven. He had been away only two minutes.

CHAPTER FIVE

KAY WAS just wondering whether he should hide the Box in his secret locker when he remembered that Abner had told the Rat to report to him at eleven at the usual place.

'I wonder,' Kay thought, 'if I could possibly be there when he reports.'

He took the Box of Delights in his hand and muttered, "If I push this to the right I can go small . . ." He pushed the knob to the right and found himself dwindling and dwindling while the furniture in his room grew vaster and vaster. There beside him just beyond the edge of the carpet was a little hole between two boards in the flooring. Without any hesitation he slipped himself down the crack and found himself in a most charming corridor, all as bright as day. It ran on and opened into a great space which had once been, as Kay knew, a secret hiding-place made by his great-grandfather. There in one corner a part had been specially polished and a mouse was roller-skating.

"Hallo, Kay," the Mouse said.

"I say," Kay said, "you know these underground places. Could I get to the Prince Rupert's Arms underground?"

"Why yes," the Mouse said, "but of course it's a bit of what you might call a peradventure, getting to the Rupert's Arms. Parts of the way there are some very terrible fellows that lie in wait."

"Do you mean cats and dogs?" Kay asked.

"Oh no, no," said the Mouse, "but a party that has only come here recently. Of course," he said, sinking his voice, "I don't say anything against them. They're awfully nice fellows and good citizens and all that but they've been away a lot. They've got foreign ways that take some getting into."

"But who are they?" Kay said.

"The chap who used to be cellarman here," the Mouse said. "I won't mention names. He went away, said he went as a marine cellarman, but if you ask me he was on the Spanish Main, under the skull and crossbones. But come along, Kay, and remember, when I put my finger to my lips that'll mean we are at the danger point."

"Tell me, before we start," Kay said, "what is the danger point?"

"Well," the Mouse said, sinking his voice, "when that one whom we named came home from the Spanish Main, he did not come alone. No, he brought Benito's crew with him, the Wolves of the Gulf, they call themselves, and they're all there, drinking rum and plotting devilry. They've brought a reign of terror into what we call the Underworld. Oh, terrible things go on every night."

"Whereabouts are they usually?" Kay asked.

"The worst place is about two-thirds of the way there," the Mouse said, "in the old Powdering Cellar under William's Vintry. We shall have to go right past it."

The Mouse began to tremble violently and turned quite white.

"Come now," Kay said, "don't be such a funk!"

The Mouse led by all sorts of strange ways towards the Rupert's Arms, along corridors, down steps, across forgotten cellars, behind a skirting-board, along an old wall and then downstairs and downstairs again to a very damp, chilly cellar where the floor and walls gleamed with salt crystals and wept tears of moisture.

"This is the Powdering Cellar," the Mouse said. "It's here that we must look out."

They stepped to one side from the Powdering Cellar and entered the thickness of the wall again. As they went on they found that it was becoming much warmer, and presently it was hot.

"What makes it hot?" Kay whispered.

"This is near the furnace of William's Vintry," the Mouse whispered, "and it's near here that they've got their quarters."

As they turned a corner, a reek of strong tobacco filled the air, there came the noise of a chair being pushed back, glasses were pounded, a drunken voice squealed with joy that Old Rum-Chops was going to sing . . . The Mouse put a warning paw on Kay's arm. "They're at it . . . just inside there," he whispered.

Indeed, just beyond them the light fell into the corridor from an open door. Kay and the Mouse paused, while within the room a most unpleasant voice broke into song. The singer may have been a little drunk, for he sometimes forgot his words and often forgot his tune, but whenever this happened the other members of the company cheered and pounded the table. These were the words of the song:

"We fly a banner all of black,
With scarlet Skull and Boneses,

> And every merchantman we take,
> We send to Davey Jones's.

Chorus gents, please . . ." And the company broke out into the chorus.

They were going on with this disgusting ditty, but the company seemed so overcome by the beauty of the words and the sentiments that they all pushed back their chairs, rose to their feet, snapped their clay pipes and started to repeat the chorus.

"Quickly, while they sing," the Mouse whispered.

As they slipped past Kay glanced in. Oh, what a terrible scene was within! There, gathered round a table, lurching, shouting, swaying and clutching at each other to keep their balance, were the Wolves of the Gulf, whom the Rat would have described as marine cellarmen. On the table around which they lurched and carolled were the remains of a hambone without any dish and a big bowl of rum punch. As Kay glanced, one of the ruffians fell forward with his head in the bowl. He splashed the rum over his head and another tried to set fire to him with a candle, but was too unsteady in his aim. All these men wore sea-boots, rough red caps and red aprons. No words can describe the villainy of their faces, all bronzed with tropical suns, purple with drink, scarlet with battle and bloated from evil living.

> "Sing diddle-diddle-dol,"

they cried. Then they drew their pistols and fired them at the ceiling so that the plaster came down with a clatter.

The Mouse plucked Kay on along the corridor. They turned a corner. There at the passage end, Kay saw the familiar figure of Rat, with a younger marine cellarman. Kay and the Mouse slipped back so as not to be seen, but they could hear Rat saying:

"Now, here we are at the door, Nephew, remember what it

was I told you. Don't you be afraid of the gent, speak out."

"I ain't afraid of no gent," Rat's nephew answered.

"Well, that's what," Rat said, and stooping down, he knocked at a little door.

"What d'you knock for?" the nephew asked.

"To show respect to the great Abner Brown," Rat answered.

Kay heard Abner's silky voice say, "Come in." Rat and his nephew passed into the room and shut the door behind them.

"This is the Rupert's Arms," the Mouse said. "If you will step up here there is a place where you can see right into the room."

Kay could see Abner in a green silk quilted dressing-gown sitting at a table. Beside him was a rather stout, stupid-looking man whom Kay took to be the man Joe, and opposite him was the foxy-faced man. Opposite Abner was a lady whose figure and bearing seemed familiar. She turned her head a moment to light a cigarette at a taper burning beside her and Kay saw that it was indeed his former governess, Sylvia Daisy Pouncer, a witch.

There was a knock at the door.

"Come in, Rat," Abner said. "Who have you got with you?"

"I make so bold as to present my nephew, Master Abner," Rat said. "Make a reverence to the gentleman."

"What's your nephew's name?" Abner asked.

"Oh, he answers to any name," Rat said. "Alf or Bert or any name."

"Now," Abner said, "what will you take, Rat?"

"Well, since I've been marine cellarman," Rat said, "I do like a drop of rum. Not because I like it, it's poison, but without it I can't stand the climate."

"A drop of rum for Rat," Abner said.

They gave Rat a tot of rum in a thimble. Rat wiped his lips with the back of his paw, tossed it off and rubbed his chest.

"That's the stuff," he said – "poison. I can feel it doing me good all the way down."

"Now, Alf," the Rat said, when he judged that he would not receive any more rum, "stand there and tell the gentlemen what you seen last night."

Alf Rat came forward and seemed much abashed at having to speak in company.

"Speak up, Alf," Abner said. "What does he say, Rat?"

"He says so many of you makes it worse than being tried, Mr Abner," Rat said.

"Well, speak for him," Abner said.

"Honoured company," Rat said, "my nephew Alf, what is here and doesn't often stand in such company, went faithful to orders to the Drop of Dew at the hour of a quarter to five yesterday. He was told to keep an eye on one that you wot of, which was C.H., what keeps a Dog B. Presently in come Two that you wot of, a man with chains and a woman without chains. C.H. pulls out a Box thing, which they look at –"

"Oh, I know all about this. You told me this last night," Abner said testily. "They agreed that the only way not guarded was out by Arthur's Camp and that this C.H. could get away at dawn by Arthur's Camp. Well, we waited for him at dawn at Arthur's Camp and got him. Tell me, Alf, when those three broke up, was the Box still in C.H.'s possession?"

"Ah, in his pocket," Alf said.

"He didn't slip it to either of the others?"

"No, they said, 'You keep it'."

"He didn't hide it in the Drop of Dew?"

"No," Alf said.

"Now listen," Abner said, "after this, you followed this C.H. all the way to Seekings House, never letting him out of your sight?"

"Never once he let him out of his sight," the Rat said.

"Let your nephew answer for himself," Abner said. "How close did you keep to him, Alf?"

"I kept him in my sight," Alf said.

"Could you see if he hid the Box on his way?"

"He had it in his pocket, he kept tapping his pocket to make sure it was there. All the way he'd tap his pocket."

"It was snowing hard. Did the snow get in your eyes?"

"No, sir."

"You must have very odd eyes," Abner growled.

"And you're sure," the man Joe said, "that on the way to Seekings he met nobody to whom he could have given the Box?"

"I take my oath on Hamlet he didn't," Alf said. "Not a soul did we pass, it being all snow, such as I never."

At this point there was a pause.

"There was another thing," said Rat, "that my nephew had to tell you if you please, gent."

"What thing? What is it?" Abner asked.

"It was about that Kay Harker, Master Abner," Rat said.

"What about him?" Abner said. "Let your nephew speak for himself. What have you got to say about this Kay Harker?"

"Well, nothing much sir," the nephew said, "except that he ought to have his head sawed off."

"What for?" Abner asked.

"Acos he's going to have a Dog give him for Christmas," the nephew said.

"You infernal young lout!" Abner said. "What do you mean, Rat, by bringing your nephew here to repeat your folly to me? Get out, the two of you! Get back to your sewer and have a bath."

Joe and the foxy-faced man took the two Rats out through the inn.

"Two infernal fools!" Abner said. "They don't seem to have a very high opinion of your ancient pupil, my dear," he said, turning to the lady.

"I don't wonder," Sylvia Daisy Pouncer said placidly. "He was a child for whom I had the utmost detestation and contempt, a thoroughly morbid, dreamy, idle muff with a low instinct for the turf, which will be his undoing later in life."

"Well now," Abner said, "the question resolves itself into this: what did that man do with the Box when those fellows let him get past them at Seekings House?"

"I felt, too late," his wife replied, "that we ought to have been there and not trusted it to those people. However, it is too late now to cry over the spilt milk."

"It's not too late to make the spillers cry," Abner said angrily. "Of all the blithering fools! He got right away under their noses."

"As for Cole," Sylvia Daisy Pouncer replied sweetly, "if he hid the Box he must have done one of two things, either hidden it on one of the bookshelves in the study at Seekings – there are old books there hardly ever disturbed, or possibly in the old cupboard in the hall there, underneath the stairs. He did not go upstairs, that I know. I have been over to Seekings in the last twenty minutes and talked to two of the little girls. They told me everything. Cole gave a marvellous conjuring performance and did not leave the library until the Tatchester choir interrupted the party. Then apparently he went into the hall and from the hall he went out with the choir. Therefore, if he hid the Box it must have been in the Library or in the hall."

"Not necessarily, my Brightness," Abner said. "While the party was singing carols in the hall he could have slipped upstairs and hidden the Box there."

"I grant that he could have, my Astuteness," Sylvia said, "but the little girls said he didn't."

"Whatever they said, the point will have to be eliminated, my Inspiration, as a matter of routine. Besides, he may not have hidden it, he may have handed it to somebody. Who were there? These Jones children and this boy, Kay Harker, your ancient pupil. I think, my Ideal, and hope that you may agree, that he would not have trusted a treasure so great to any child whom he had not seen before that afternoon."

"Well then, there remains the guardian," Sylvia said: "This Caroline Louisa."

"Cole would have regarded her as the mistress of the house, certainly," Abner said, "and as a woman to be trusted. He could have handed it to her and whispered to her to keep it for him."

"Your imagination is Shakespearean," Sylvia Daisy said.

"Therefore," Abner said, "we shall have to take steps about Madam Caroline Louisa."

"May a weak woman make a suggestion, my starlike Abner?" Sylvia said. "Is it not more likely that he handed it to the Bishop, the Precentor, the Archdeacon or one of the Canons? You see, he was really in luck. There he was, unexpectedly in the midst of the most respectable company in the country, everyone of which could be trusted to any amount."

"It is only too likely, my Empress. And whichever of the Cathedral staff had it would have called in all the others and they'd have put the Box in the Cathedral treasure vaults. And you know what kind of vaults those are: Guy Fawkes and his powder wouldn't get through those. That's where the Box is now, depend upon it."

"My dear," his wife said, "I think you look a little too much on the gloomy side of things. At this time, so near to Christmas, the whole Cathedral staff is working overtime and normal procedures are in abeyance. I think it very likely that the Bishop, or whoever it was, put the Box into a drawer in his dressing-table among his collars and his handkerchiefs and thought no more about it."

Abner shook his head. "My priceless Pearl," he said, "my blue and yellow Sapphire, if I may call you so, I wish I could think it. But if Cole didn't hide it, he gave it to someone, that's sure. That's the first point to settle, and our Routine will still find out which . . ."

"Will you ask The Boy?" Sylvia asked, making a sign with her hand.

"I can't wait till I get home," he answered. "With luck we ought to know before then. Look here, Sylvia, I'm tempted to get rid of Charles, with his infernal 'ha-ha, what'."

"Oh no, my Emerald," she said. "He is one of our most precious workers. Get rid of Charles? Never. Whatever for?"

"He was specially charged to nobble and scrobble Cole," Abner said. "He let Cole go right past him with the goods on him, with his Toby Dog in his pocket and the Punch and Judy show on his shoulder. Could a prize imbecile have been blinder or sillier, I ask you?"

"My Abner," Sylvia said, "you are unjust to our Charles. The terrier may have been in Cole's pocket. Many terriers are very small. No doubt the show was also folded up very tight and not to be seen. Of course it was. How unjust of you to blame poor Charles. You must never, never think of getting rid of Charles. I repeat, my Emerald, never think of it. He did his duty well in the terrible night of storm and was deceived by a ruse. Get your Routine to work by all means, but then get home and ask The Boy."

"The Routine is all at work," he said. "As to Charles, I shall follow my own judgment."

"My Topaz and my Diamond," Sylvia said, "can you not see that Charles is our only buffer against the stupidity and the craft of Joe? Can you not see that Charles is the only friend we have? But enough, my Idol, you do see – I see you see. Now as to this child, Maria Jones, whose ways you like – I admit, she sounds most promising. Remember that Cole may have given the Box to her."

"I remember," Abner said, "but even so that would be a point in her favour. She must be here now. Shall I ring for them to bring her?"

"Do, my own Abby," Sylvia said.

Kay saw Abner stretch out his left hand and press a button in the middle of the table. An electric bell rang somewhere below in the house. Almost immediately the foxy-faced man and another curate, whom Kay had never before seen, entered with little Maria.

[53]

"Ah, Miss Maria," Abner said, "good morning. It was most kind of you to come. Someone was saying that you were very much interested in stained glass. We were making up a little party to go over to St. Griswold's this morning, looking at the glass and being back at Seekings before tea. Would you care to come along? Oh, by the way, you haven't been introduced: this lady is Mrs Brown."

"Oh," Maria said, nodding at Mrs Brown, "it's rather a mouldy lot of glass, isn't it, at St. Griswold's?"

"In the main church, yes," the foxy-faced man said, "but in the Lady Chapel . . ."

"It's a pretty mouldy thing, English glass, if you ask me," Maria said.

"Well, I think you will find this isn't English glass," the foxy-faced man said.

"Well, my dear," Mrs Brown said, "before we start would you like to run back to Seekings and leave word that you will be out until teatime?"

"Oh no," Maria said, "thanks. They know that I can look after myself. I've generally got a pistol or two on me and I'm a dead shot with both hands."

"How you must enjoy the quiet atmosphere of school," Abner said.

"School!" Maria said. "They know better than to try that game on me. I've been expelled from three and the head-mistresses still swoon when they hear my name breathed."

"I count it a great honour," Abner said, "to entertain so distinguished an ornament of her sex. Then, we will start, shall we? We will get to the Bear's Paw at Tatchester for lunch – the place is still famous for duck patty."

They moved out of the room, Mrs Brown with her hand on Maria's shoulder. Kay, crouched at the spy-hole, tried to cry out, "Don't go with them, Maria! They're up to no good. They're the gang," but being tiny as he was, his voice made a little reedy squeak like the buzzing of a fly.

"Back now," he said to the Mouse, "back now to Seekings as fast as ever we can go."

At this instant, round the corner of the corridor came a party of the Wolves of the Gulf. They had been drinking more rum since Kay had passed them and there they were, pot-valiant, swinging lighted lanterns in their left hands and brandishing cutlasses in their right. Kay heard one of them say, "There are their footsteps in the dust – two of them, a mouse and another – and we'll grind their bones to make our bread."

"Yes," another said, "we'll cut 'em into little collops. There they are!"

"Where?" said another. "I'll eat their livers fried!"

Kay saw their gleaming teeth, their red eyes and their flashing cutlass edges. "Give me your hand, Mouse," he said. Quickly he caught the Mouse's hand and with his other hand twiddled the knob on the magic Box that he might go swiftly and instantly the two of them were plucked up into the air and whirled past the Wolves of the Gulf back to Seekings.

"Kay," Susan was saying from the other side of the door, "do you know where Jemima is?"

"No," he said. "What do you want Jemima for?"

"Well," she said, "I was out in the street buying Christmas presents and Maria got into a car with some total strangers at the Rupert's Arms and she has gone off with them, and she knows she is absolutely forbidden to get into cars with total strangers."

"What sort of a car was it?" Peter asked.

"Oh, it was a big, rather old dark car. I didn't like the look of the strangers at all, the two of them were dressed like curates."

"I expect it will be all right," Kay said. He did not think it would be all right, he was very much worried and wished that Caroline Louisa was there. As he went downstairs, Ellen met him.

"Oh, Master Kay," she said, "I didn't hear you come in. There has been a message from your guardian. She'll be here tonight by the eight-seven, she says, while you're all at Tatchester at the Punch and Judy show."

"Oh good, I am glad," he said. "Is her brother well then?"

"Much better, she said, "Master Kay."

"Oh, splendid."

He called the others into the study and told them how Maria had gone with Abner and the gangsters.

"She'll be all right," Peter said. "Maria can look after herself."

"It is like Maria," Jemima said, "to go plunging off with any scoundrels who come along with a suggestion."

"I say, it's rather sport," Susan said. "Supposing they say, 'Miss Maria Jones, you will either join our gang or go down the oubliette for ever'?"

"I pity any gangster who talks like that to Maria," Peter said.

Still feeling uneasy and wishing that he knew what to do, Kay went round to the Rupert's Arms to speak to the proprietress, Mrs Calamine.

"Could you tell me, please, who the clergymen were who were here this morning?"

"Those, Master Kay?" she said. "That was the Reverend Doctor Boddledale, with his wife and chaplain and private secretaries. He is the head of the Missionary and Theological Training College at Chesters in the Chester Hills."

"I thought he was named Mr Brown."

"Oh no, Master Kay, he's well known and a very holy man, and his lady, Mrs Boddledale – oh, she does wear lovely jewels. She reminds me of someone I've seen somewhere. It's always on the tip of my tongue who."

Kay knew who, but did not say.

By this time, a steady warm rain had set in from the west and it was too wet for the children to play outdoors after lunch.

Kay thought, 'If Maria does not come back by dark I'll go to the police about her, though somehow I don't think the Inspector will be much help in the business.'

The darkness came before four o'clock that evening and Maria had not returned. Kay slipped round to the Inspector of Police and told his story and his suspicions.

"Have no fears, Master Kay," the Inspector said. "The Reverend Doctor Boddledale is a pillar of the Church and respectability. I've sung in the Glee Club with him time and time again – a very sweet tenor, Master Kay. Now depend upon it, Master Kay, you have come home, if I may say so, a little faint from the strain of learning. I often notice it in young fellows just back from school. Your young friend is in good hands, believe me, and she'll be back, you may be sure. Or, wait one moment, wasn't you to be tonight at the Punch and Judy show at Tatchester Palace?"

"Yes," Kay said, "I was. We were just going to start."

"And wasn't Miss Maria to be there?" the Inspector said. "Well then, you say she's been to St. Griswold's to look at that old glass: why should she come back all the way to Seekings? She'll have stopped in Tatchester, depend upon it, had tea there and gone on direct to the Palace."

"I hadn't thought of that," Kay said. "Of course that's very likely to have happened."

"Ah," the Inspector said, "we in the Law, Master Kay, we've got a maxim, 'It's the easy explanation that never occurs'. You think all's battle, murder and sudden death, and all the time it's only a tyre getting a puncture. You get that good guardian of yours to see you take a strong posset every night. But you young folks in this generation, you don't know what a posset is. Well, a posset," said the Inspector, "is a jorum of hot milk and in that hot milk you put a hegg and you put a spoonful of treacle and you put a grating of nutmeg and you stir 'em well up and you get into bed and then you take 'em down hot. And a posset like that, taken overnight, it will make a new man of you, Master Kay, while now you're all worn down with learning."

Kay thanked him and hurried back to Seekings, where all the children were clamouring for him to buck up or they would be late for the Punch and Judy show.

"It's all right," Kay said, "we shall be in lots of time. It's not much of a run to Tatchester and there's a Roman road most of the way."

They got into the car and in spite of the slush upon the roads they were soon at Tatchester Palace, where the Bishop and his sister gave them a royal tea.

CHAPTER SIX

"Please," Kay said to the Bishop, "can I talk to the Punch and Judy man?"

"I am afraid not," the Bishop said. "He asked specially that the children should not talk to him either before or after the performance. He is an old man and suffering rather from his throat."

"But it is Cole Hawlings, isn't it?" Kay asked. "The old man who was at Seekings last night?"

"Oh yes," the Bishop said, "it's Cole Hawlings."

Presently, they were all taken to the room in which the performance was to be given. Kay thought, 'Now I'll be able to speak to him,' but in this he was disappointed. It was a long room, once the guestroom of the pilgrims, with a stage at the end almost covered with a curtain and with the Punch and Judy theatre standing on it. The performance took place on the other side of the curtain and there was no chance whatever for him to speak to Old Cole. It seemed to be exactly the theatre that Cole had used and the Toby dog was an Irish terrier, but at the end of the play, when Kay called, "Barney, Barney," the dog did not answer to his name. Kay wondered several times during the performance whether the performer's voice was quite that of Cole.

When the curtain fell Kay's hopes of speaking to the old man were at an end, for the Bishop at once said, "And now, everybody, I want you to move into the next room behind you, to dance round our Christmas tree and receive your gifts."

In the midst of the next room was the biggest and most glorious Christmas tree that had ever been seen in Tatchester. It stood in a monstrous half-barrel full of what looked like real snow stuck about with holly and mistletoe. At the top of this great green fir tree was a globe of green light set about with fiery white rays for the Christmas Star.

The boughs were laden with the most exquisite gifts: whistles, drums, tops of different kinds, whips, trumpets, swords, pop-guns, pistols that fired caps and others which fired corks and many dolls and teddy-bears for the little ones. For the older boys there were railways with signals and switches and passenger trains and goods trains, some of which went by steam and others by clockwork. There were aeroplanes which you could wind up so that they would fly about the room. There were farmyards with cocks and hens which really pecked and cows which waggled their heads. There were zoos with all sorts of animals and aquariums with all sorts of fish. Then there were mechanical toys, men boxing or wrestling and boxes of soldiers with cavalry and cannons, bricks and Meccano and all sorts of adventure books and fairy books. For the girls there were needle-boxes with silver thimbles and cases of needles, necklaces, bangles and brooches. There were boxes of chocolates, candied fruits and great glass bottles of barley sugar, raspberry drops, peppermint drops and acid drops. Then for both girls and boys there were toy boats, some with sails and some with clockwork engines. Hanging from the boughs here and there were white and scarlet stockings, all bulging with chocolate creams done up in silver paper.

All round this marvellous tree were wonderful crackers, eighteen inches long. The Bishop made all the children stand in a double rank round the tree, each with one end of a cracker in each hand. The musicians struck up a tune and they danced in the double rank three times round the Christmas tree. Then the Bishop gave the word and they pulled the crackers, which went off with a bang together, like cannons. And then, suddenly, Kay remembered that he had not thought about little Maria since he left the Police Inspector.

'Good heavens!' he thought. 'Maria isn't here. What shall I do?' He went up to the Bishop's sister and asked her if Maria had been there.

"No," she said, "no. And the Bishop said just now to me, 'I'm sorry not to see little Maria here. She may think I bear malice for the smashing up of my car that time but indeed that isn't so. I should have loved to have her here.'"

"D'you mind if I telephone?" Kay said. He went down and telephoned to Ellen.

"No," Ellen said, "Miss Maria hasn't come back."

"By the way," Kay called, "we shall be a little late in getting away from here. Will you ask the Rupert's Arms to send a car to meet the eight-seven?"

Ellen said she would. Presently, the evening came to an end and all the happy children got ready to go away. Just as they were crowding into the hall, going off in instalments as the cars came for them, the butler came to the Bishop with a look of great gravity on his face. Kay was standing close beside the Bishop and heard him say, "What is it, Rogers?" And the butler replied, "I am sorry to tell Your Grace that during the performance burglars have been in every room of the Palace.

They have turned the place just topsy-turvy, Your Grace."

"Indeed," the Bishop said. "Warn the police, Rogers. I will be with you in a moment, as soon as my young friends have gone."

"If you please, Your Grace," Kay said, "do you think I might say goodbye to the Punch and Judy man?"

"I am afraid he has gone," the Bishop said. "Somebody in an old car came for him as soon as the performance was over."

Kay thanked the Bishop for their glorious treat and they were soon in the car, driving home in the slush.

"Well, I do hope," said Kay, "that Maria hasn't been in the burglary with the gang. It would be just like her to do a thing like that."

"Maria won't have had a hand in it," Susan said, "except to collar all the swag and bring it back to its owners."

When they reached home there was no news of little Maria, but in some strange way the news of the burglary had reached Ellen. She greeted the children with, "I do hope the burglars didn't frighten you."

"No, they didn't," Kay said. "Has Miss Maria turned up?"

"No, not yet, Master Kay," Ellen said.

"Is my guardian back?" he asked.

"No, Master Kay," Ellen said. "The Rupert's Arms man met the eight-seven but she didn't come by that train and there's no other train from London tonight."

"Did any message come from her?"

"No," Ellen said, "I telephoned through to the number you gave. She'd started off to catch that train."

"Well," Kay said, "I suppose all the trains are upset, partly with Christmas and partly with the snow. She may have gone a certain distance and then had to come on by car."

"It may have been something like that," Ellen said.

"Well, I don't know," Kay said. "Do you think I had better speak to the Inspector of Police?"

Then he remembered the Inspector's maxim.

"Ellen," he said, "can you make possets?"

"Yes, Master Kay," she said, "I can."

"Well, I wish you'd make me a big one," he said, "because I'm feeling very miserable."

He went up to bed and found Peter already tucked in, reading a murder story. Kay got into bed and presently Ellen brought him a posset in a mug. He drank it down, thinking that the Inspector certainly knew a good thing—the comfort seemed to tingle through him, putting an end to his miseries.

When Kay woke up the fire was almost out, but the moonlight shone in through the open curtains, and outside on the hard asphalt of the walks round the house came the clank of weapons and the stamp of feet marching in time. A trumpet blew and a stern voice cried, "The Wolf Guard setting out for Duke's Heath! Guard against the Wolves!"

Kay looked out of the window and there he saw in the moonlight a pack of armed men with bronze scale-armour, shields on their left arms, short swords by their sides and two short spears each.

"Are you coming, Kay?" the Captain said. Duke's Heath was a couple of miles away, but it seemed to Kay much too good a chance to miss.

"Yes, of course I'm coming," he said.

He took his precious Box, which had been under his pillow, and in a minute he was out of the house.

Kay thought that the officer beside whom he was marching was very good-looking and agreeable. He was young, pale, with quick eyes and black hair and some of his dash was in his men too. They marched like one man, with snap and swagger.

"Will you tell me who you are, please?" Kay asked.

"We?" the young officer said. "We're the smartest squad in the finest cohort in the star wing of the crack legion of the whole Imperial Roman Army. Search it where you will, you'll not find anything anywhere to touch or come near the Blue and White Stripers of the Tatchester Toms."

"I suppose not," Kay said. "And are you going to camp at Duke's Moor?"

"No, no," the man said. "We're the Wolf-guard passing that way with the mails. We go on to the frontier."

"Are the Wolves very bad?" Kay asked.

"So, so," the man said. "It's best to keep your eyes skinned. Duke's Moor is none too good a place. There are some of the old lot there who used to hold Chester Hills."

"There's a Roman camp at Chester Hills," Kay said.

"There had need to be," the officer said.

"Were you ever fighting there?" Kay asked.

"You'd call it so," he said. "A bad place and bad people. Men disappeared – sentry after sentry – and were never seen again. You see, it's limestone country, all honeycombed with caves and these Wolves, as we call them, were all underground. It cost us a lot of men to get them out of it."

They marched so swiftly that very soon they were out of the town in the open fields, with Duke's Moor already black to their right front.

"You're looking for a friend, and if I were you I'd wait here for him. Don't cross the brook. Some of the Wolves may be out on the other side and they're none too good."

"You mean men wolves?" Kay said.

"See now," the officer said, "that flat bit near the brook. Well, on that flat bit, one of our posts saw a calf come out in the moonlight to feed, just one of these wild white calves that you see. Nothing odd in that: the calf fed and scratched and stamped like any other, but the posts noticed that it was always drawing nearer. At last one of the men didn't like the look of it so he flung a stone and called, 'Get out of that!' and at once the calf tossed off its skin and charged the post, hurt one man and got away with two spears. It was two of these young Wolves under a cow-skin. That was only three years ago, just here. They're none too good, the Wolves."

The squad's music, a strange kind of horn and drum, broke

out into a march and the squad stepped out to it with a stamp and jingle. Soon even the noise of the march was gone. Kay was alone near the swollen brook and the dripping trees of the dingle. The night was now black as a pocket and there in the blackness, oh horror, was a white calf moving towards him, just as the Roman had described. Then the moon shone out again and he saw it was a white lady who held her hand in a peculiar way so that he could see a large ring with a glittering St. Andrew's Cross on it. She was the Lady who had been outside Bob's shop, waiting for the message.

"Come, Kay," she said, "you must not stay here, for the Wolves are Running. Listen!"

The midnight was still enough, save for the babble of the brook and the occasional running patter of drops from the ash trees. Now above these noises, from out to the north by the straw yards, came the cry of Wolves in pack, 'All mad,' Kay thought, 'like the bark of foxes but much more awful.'

"Come with me," she said, giving him her hand.

As he took it he felt himself lifted from the grass and glided beside her up the stream to a hollow oak of great age whose mighty shell was alive still.

"There are the Wolves," she said. "Look!"

There in the moonlight, racing over the grass to them, were the Wolves in pack with their ruffs up and their eyes glaring. The oak tree opened behind Kay and the woman stepped within, drawing Kay with her. Instantly they were within the quiet of the tree in a room panelled with living oak wood and hung with tapestries of oak leaves in which the birds were alive. Kay marvelled, for the birds came out of the tapestries and perched upon his hands. "They want some strawberries," the woman said, "won't you give them some?"

Out of a little door in one of the walls a red squirrel came cocking with very bright eyes. He carried in his forepaws a cabbage leaf heaped with strawberries. He hopped down to the table and offered the leaf to Kay, who took the berries and gave them to the birds. It was charming to have the little birds' claws upon the fingers.

"Now Kay would like some supper," the woman said, "for indeed, Kay, things are not going too well when the Wolves have the best of us underground and are still Running."

Indeed, they were Running, sweeping past the tree with every kind of shriek and madness.

"They have taken Cole," she said, "they have taken Maria and they will take others, but don't lose courage, Kay, even if the Wolves are Running. You will beat the Wolves, won't you, Kay?"

Kay said he would and at once there he was back in his bed at Seekings, in daylight, with Peter saying, "It's about time you woke. You've been snoring like a stuck pig. Have you had a nightmare?"

When he came down to breakfast there was no letter from his guardian but there was a newspaper and the children pounced upon this for news of the burglary at the Palace:

REGRETTABLE INCIDENT AT
TATCHESTER PALACE

We are informed that a serious and very successful burglary was carried out at Tatchester Palace last evening. According to the Bishop's laudable custom before Christmas the Palace was the scene last night of a large children's party with a Christmas tree and other festivities. While these were in progress the burglars, who, it is thought, were assisted by someone secreted in the Palace, went through the guestrooms and escaped with considerable booty. It is understood that dramatic developments may be expected shortly.

"But that's what they always say," Peter said.

Kay was very much worried about Maria being still absent,

although Maria's brothers and sisters said that she would be all right. "She always falls on her feet," they said. "Don't you worry about Maria." But Kay did worry. As soon as breakfast was over he went across to see the Inspector of Police.

"So, you haven't seen Miss Maria," the Inspector said. "Ha, that doesn't look so well, but you leave the matter in my hands, Master Kay, and I'll make what enquiries are called for. And your guardian, I hear, hasn't come back."

"No," Kay said, "that's another point. She ought to have been back, she started out yesterday to catch a certain train and she didn't come by it. We've had no word from her since."

"You leave the matter to the bloodhounds of the Law, Master Kay, and depend upon it, information will be received."

Kay was cheered by his confident manner and by his repeating, "The simple explanation is always the last thing thought of."

When he reached Seekings Ellen said, "Oh, Master Kay, your guardian's brother has rung up. There was so much fog and such a crowd at the station yesterday that she didn't start but went back to her brother. She may be back tomorrow."

"Well, that's a jolly good thing," Kay said, much cheered by the news. As he glanced out of the window towards King Arthur's Camp he saw in the fields below the camp the gleam of water. He ran down at once to the others.

"I say," he said, "it's splendid – the floods are out. We'll go for a mud-lark. We'll get out all our ships and sail them on the floods."

Both Peter and he had received ships from the Bishop's Christmas tree.

"We'll provision them with almonds, raisins and chocolates," said Kay, "and we'll all take long sticks so as to poke them off if they get stuck anywhere. And we'll take sandwiches, cakes and hard-boiled eggs and we won't come back till teatime."

"I've got some lovely little things that would do for the ships," said Susan. "In the stocking they gave me from the tree there were those little tiny wooden barrels filled with Hundreds and Thousands. They were just the sort of barrels to go in the ships."

She fetched the barrels and they divided them up among the ships and put raisins and currants and bits of biscuit in each barrel.

"I vote," Jemima said, "that the other barrels should be filled with ham, which we will pretend is salt-pork."

"They don't take salt-pork any more," Peter said. "They take pemmican, which is beef chopped up with fat and raisins and chocolate and beer and almonds and ginger and stuff. It must be a sickening mess but it's very nourishing. It's supposed to be what the Ancient Britons had. They could take a piece as big as a currant and live on it for a week."

"You'd better have some anchors," Jemima said. "All ships have anchors, otherwise they wouldn't be able to stop."

"You've got to be jolly careful with anchors with ships as little as these," Kay said. "Very often if you try anchoring little ships like these, the anchor will pull them right underneath the water."

They went out to the woodshed to get long sticks for poking off the ships if they got stuck and then away they went in bright, sunny weather, with the noise of running water everywhere. When they came to the meadows there were pools in all the hollows and many of the mole-hills were bubbling up water like running springs. Kay had the Box of Delights in his inner pocket and sometimes poked his hand inside to be sure that it was there.

Presently all was ready and away the ships went downstream with the children following, shouting and cheering and poking them clear of the banks with their sticks.

When they had gone about half a mile down the stream Susan, who was looking up at the sky, said, "There's an aeroplane – no, two."

The others didn't see the aeroplanes at first but then saw them like two bright specks against a dark cloud. "It's odd we didn't hear them," Susan said.

They went on with their ships, paddling in the water, getting very wet and enjoying themselves so much that they forgot about all other things, till Kay suddenly saw a shadow running across the field in front of him and looking up, saw two aeroplanes circling silently overhead. "I say, look at the aeroplanes," he said. "Absolutely silent!"

Kay didn't say so, but the thought flashed through his mind that the aeroplanes were there after them; but the other thought also flashed that no aeroplane would dare to land on ground so rotten with springs as that low-lying field.

"They're going to land," Susan said. "They're coming down by the copse there."

"Bring the ships in to the banks," Kay said.

There were some old willow trees where he was standing. Climbing up one of them he saw four men getting out of the aeroplanes.

"They've got pistols and ropes," he said, "and they're coming towards us. I think it would be wise to get out of the way."

"Do you think they're after us?" Susan said.

"Who'd be coming after us with pistols and ropes?" Jemima said. "They're probably mole-catchers coming to set traps."

"When did you ever hear of mole-catchers coming in aeroplanes with pistols?" said Peter.

"What shall we do?" said Susan. "Shall we run to the mill or the farm?"

"They'd beat us to either of those," Kay said.

"Then what can we do?" Susan asked.

"Well, I've got here," Kay said, "a sort of magic dodge. If we all hold hands while I touch a button on it we shall shrink into little tiny creatures and then we'll pop on board our ships and go down the stream."

They held hands, he twiddled the little button and instantly each one of them felt brighter and lighter than ever before. The earth seemed to shoot up and become enormous and there they were, clambering on board their gigantic ships. They cast loose the strings which tied them to the bank and away they sailed downstream.

Just as the ships went round the bend, the four men came in sight, close to the bank. It was plain that each man had two long pistols stuck in his belt and they were coiling lassos ready for a throw. The ships went gaily down the millstream into the mill-race. At the mill-race came a roaring and terrible torrent, down which the ships plunged so swiftly that they were through it before they had time to be afraid. In an instant they were in quiet water out of all the currents, with the ships' sides gently rubbing against the roots of an elm tree which grew in the high bank. Kay and Peter hooked the anchors onto some of the roots of the tree and they secured the ships alongside each other.

CHAPTER SEVEN

"AND NOW," Kay said, "I vote we have our pemmican and decide what to do next."

At this moment a little voice sounded from up above. "Hullo, you people," it said. "Come indoors, you can have your feast in here. I'll let down a cage to hoist you up."

They saw a little fieldmouse leaning over a platform which projected from the trunk of the elm. Presently the little cage came dangling down from a crane and the Fieldmouse said, "Not more than two of you at one time."

Peter and Jemima got in and the little mouse went to a winch and set the works going. Quickly the cage was up at the platform. Then it was sent down for Kay and Susan.

"Now let's lunch," said the Fieldmouse. They got out their provisions: pemmican, ham and the rest, and the Fieldmouse produced some blackberry wine and beechnut loaves which Susan toasted at the fire. While they were feasting in this happy way they heard a great clumping noise outside.

"That's men," the Fieldmouse said. "They might be elephants the noise they make." Almost at once the men began to talk.

"Well," one man said, "they seem to have got away from us. They must have come downstream under cover of the banks somehow. We'd have seen them if they'd gone upstream, because there aren't any banks."

"If they've gone into the stream the flood must have got them," said another.

The first one said, "There's nothing like children for leading one a dance – little devils! I thought you were making a mistake bringing both the 'planes down and losing sight of them."

"How would it be to look under the bridge there?" one said. "They'd time to get to the bridge."

The voices and footsteps moved away.

When they had gone, the Fieldmouse said, "Perhaps you'd like to see some of the wonders of this tree." He threw up a shutter in the wall, revealing a little cage like the one in which he had hoisted them from the ships. "You see," he said, "I have to have a good many places like this. If I hear someone coming whom I don't want, you understand – I name no names, but there are several round here, uncertain sort of chaps and you can never tell in a place like this – now that I've got the lifts fixed I nip into one of these places. Just step in here, will you, and I press a button and up we go."

The cage shot upwards. When it stopped they were amazed to find that they were right at the very top of the great elm tree. Close to them was an old rook's nest, looking like a mass of black timbers, big as a church. Just beyond it, on a twig, was a rook swaying in the sun, his back glistening purple. "Dangerous chaps, those," the Fieldmouse said. "I keep out of their way as a rule. Now here is one of the slides."

They slithered down and found themselves in a bare corridor. The Fieldmouse opened a little shutter and told them to look within, to the hollow of the tree. They saw a multitude of bees which had almost filled the hollow with their honeycombs. Although it was winter they were moving, making the place drone like a thrashing-machine. The place smelt as though all the summer was still there, with lime-blossom and bean-blossom. "This is a fine place on a cold winter night," the Fieldmouse said, "curled up in a blanket and letting the bees drone you to sleep."

"Oh, and then," he said, "there are the jackdaws. Very odd chaps, the jackdaws. If you will look in the corner here you will see the kind of things they bring."

In a corner, near an opening, where a knot in the wood had fallen, was a heap of stuff which sparkled. There was a lady's little gold watch, two rings set with brilliants, a pin with a fox's-head top, a bit of quartz which gleamed, two scraps of Roman glass, iridescent from being in the earth for eighteen hundred years, the red cut-glass stopper of a bottle, a broken glass marble with a coloured spiral in it, a bit of brass chain and a crystal seal set in gold. "They just bring these things in and leave them," the Fieldmouse said. "Queer chaps."

"Before we go, just come up this stair. You will see a sight."

They crept up a little stair and looked into what seemed like a cavern, within which, just below them, a big white owl was perched fast asleep, gurgling and growling. Peter dropped a bit of bark on to him. He half opened an eye and gurgled back to sleep again. "He's the oldest thing around here," the Fieldmouse said. "He remembers when this tree was a sprig and when the Very Good People were here. He makes my blood run cold, he's so old, and his place is a graveyard of my relations, if the truth were known."

He opened another little door, a trap-door in the floor. The children could see a long shoot leading downwards.

"It's perfectly safe," the Fieldmouse said, "nothing but weed and moss to fall on, you can't hurt yourself." With that he let himself drop and the children followed. "Now this," the Fieldmouse said, as they got to their feet in a strange room, "this is a part of the tree that's really worth seeing."

The room in which they were had been a music room but it was dusty and cobwebby, unused for many years. "Now this, you see, is a part that was made by the Very Good People, who don't come here any more."

"D'you mean Fairies?" Susan asked.

"No, Very, Very Good People," the Fieldmouse said, "very clever, very beautiful and very wise. But they went away. I don't know the rights of it," the Fieldmouse added. "It isn't wise to talk about those People, but of course everybody knows they were Very, Very Good."

He led the way out of the music room to a staircase hung with tapestries showing countless little people carrying coloured baubles to a queen of extraordinary beauty who sat upon a mushroom.

"Now, this place," the Fieldmouse said, when they reached the foot of the stairs, "I don't quite like going into, but it's so beautiful I can't keep from it." He opened a big door into a great room which seemed to fill the whole hollow of the tree. The walls were hung with banners and with portraits of extraordinary, brilliant people, whose eyes seemed to move in their painted heads. At the end of the room was a dais with a throne and in front of the throne a table on which lay an ivory horn. Underneath the horn, written in letters of flame which flickered to and fro, were the words:

> "He that dares blow must blow me thrice
> Or feed th'outrageous cockatrice."

"Oh, I would love to blow," Kay said, "just to see what would happen. What is a cockatrice?"

"Don't!" Susan said. "Anything might happen. A cockatrice

is a fearful thing, like a cock and a cobra mixed."

"I wouldn't touch the thing, sir," the Fieldmouse said. "Oh no, you mustn't think of doing that, nobody's done that, even the Owl wouldn't dare to do a thing like that, why, the Fox wouldn't."

"Do blow it, Kay," Peter said. "Just for a lark."

They could see that the Fieldmouse was in a twitter with terror, but Kay picked up the horn, put it to his lips and blew. He blew once and a strange noise as sweet as the winter singing of the storm-cock came from the ivory. With a little tinkle and clack all the frames fell from the portraits on the walls. The little mouse shrieked with terror and got underneath the table.

Kay blew a second time. This time the note was louder and stronger, like the first calling of the cuckoo when he comes in April. The children heard a sort of gasp of breath from the portraits on the walls and all the figures of the portraits turned their heads and looked at Kay.

"Oh Kay, they're looking at you," Susan said.

"Never mind," Kay said. The Fieldmouse had by this time got his head underneath the carpet.

Kay blew a third blast and at this all the lights in the room burned out a thousandfold more brightly and the blast of the horn became like the song of all the birds in June singing together, with a noise of the little silver bells that hung on the sleeves of Herne the Hunter. And at this all the beautiful people in the portraits stepped down into the room. The portraits over the door were those of a King and a Queen. As the children turned they saw this King and Queen advancing through the company towards the throne. They took their seats and all the company burst out into singing. The children stared in amazement, for they had never seen people so beautiful as these, all exquisitely lovely and so delicate and so swift. Some were winged, but all could move with the speed of thought and they were clad in the colours of the dewdrops in the sun. And as they sang, countless other marvellous people of the sort thronged in through the doors and at once they fell to dancing to music so beautiful, so moving, that to listen to it was almost too great a joy. Some beautiful little men moved up to Jemima and Susan and asked them to dance; princesses caught Kay and Peter by the hand and swept them into the dance and as they danced they all seemed to understand what it is that makes the planets dance about the sun and the great stars keep their place in the constellations as they move for ever in the heavens.

When the dance ended the King of the Fairies said, "Friends, the long enchantment has been brought to an end. What can we do for Kay, who has ended it for us?"

The Queen of the Fairies said, "We will grant him the power to come again into Fairyland on one day in every year."

At this moment Kay heard again that heavy tread which had so disturbed him at lunch. "Kay's enemies," the King of the Fairies said. At once the lights went out, the Fairies vanished.

"Abner won't be too pleased," said a man's voice, "when he hears the result of today. I told you one of the aeroplanes had better keep up in the air to observe."

"Oh, you told us a lot, didn't you?" another voice said.

"Blessed if I haven't got pins and needles all over me, crouching there by that bridge," one of the men said as they moved off.

"And I have," another said.

"It isn't pins and needles," said Susan, "the Fairies are pricking them. Look there."

Indeed, down at the tree-foot the children saw countless little Fairies jabbing and tweaking the men. They looked like little fireflies darting to and from the great dark figures.

"Blessed if we haven't all got rheumatics waiting like this," a man growled. "Come on, we'll get home before we're paralysed."

After this the men hurried away.

"I say, it's quite dark," said Kay. "I'm awfully sorry that we've stayed so long."

When they had said goodbye the Fieldmouse opened the front door at the foot of the elm. The children joined hands, Kay pressed the button of his Box and they resumed their shapes and fished out the boats from the hollow of the elm-tree roots.

"Come along," Kay said, "we'd better hurry."

As they came into the garden of Seekings they saw that the house was lit up at every window and the doors wide open.

"Good heavens," Kay said, "look at this!"

The study and hall had been turned topsy-turvy, carpets taken up and rolled back, every drawer and cupboard ransacked, every book moved on the shelves. While they were marvelling, Ellen and Jane came back. They said they had been called away to look to Ellen's mother who was said to be very ill, but when they reached her they found her never better.

"Well, while you've been away a gang's ransacked the house," Kay said. "Do look at what they've done. They don't seem to have taken much."

"Oh Master Kay," Ellen said, "whatever shall we do? Whatever will your guardian think?"

'This is more of Abner's Routine,' Kay thought, going up to his room which reeked of strong plug tobacco. "I know who has been in here," he said. "Those Wolves of the Gulf have been in – that's the plug tobacco they were smoking in the cellar."

After supper, as the four children were sitting round the study fire, the hall door opened and somebody came in.

"I wonder if that's my guardian," Kay said.

He went into the hall and there was Maria. "I say, Maria, I am glad to see you," he said. "Where on earth have you been?"

"I don't know where I've been," Maria said. "I've been scrobbled just like a greenhorn. I knew what it would be, not taking a pistol. Well, I pity them if I ever get near them again. They won't scrobble Maria Jones a second time!"

"But what on earth happened to you?" Peter said. "You aren't usually the one to get scrobbled. Who scrobbled you?"

"I don't know," she said. "I went with those clergymen people and looked at the stained glass and then we had lunch. It was the only good part of the proceedings – I'm very partial to duck patty. Then presently they went out and it was beastly wet, as you know, so I thought I'd take a taxi. Taxi came, I got in, 'Drive me to Market Square, please,' I said. Presently I saw it was going a different way, so I said, 'Market Square!' The driver said, 'The road's up, Miss, got to go this way,' and at that he put on speed and a sort of cast-iron curtain came down over all the windows. There I was, shut up in a black box, going about fifty miles an hour right out of Tatchester. I beat on the shutters but I might have spared my strength, the car went faster and faster and at last, from the queer lurch it gave, I knew that it was up in the air."

"Oh, that's rot," Peter said. "How can a car go up in the air? And a Tatchester taxi! Poor old crocks tied together with boot-lace!"

"This wasn't a taxi," Maria said. "I don't know what it was – some marvellous invention – but it was an aeroplane, or a car that became an aeroplane. And we were making hardly any noise."

"It couldn't have been an aeroplane, then," Peter said. "You must have an enormously powerful engine to go fast, so of course you have noise."

"I say," Kay said, "you are in luck, Maria. What happened then?"

"Well," she said, "presently I felt the aeroplane dipping down. Then it touched the ground and went bumping over grass for a while and then I heard it scraunch on gravel. Then I heard a sort of door clang to behind it, the shutter went up on one side, the door of the thing opened and I saw a light along a little passage. I walked towards the light and came into a small room with white-washed walls and no window. It was lit from the ceiling about twelve feet up. I was no sooner in the room than a great iron door shut up behind me, and there I was, shut in. Then high up on the wall an iron shutter slid to one side and there was an iron grille with a lady's face and a very silky female voice said, 'Miss Maria Jones, please forgive any inconvenience we may have caused you in bringing you here and above all don't be afraid.' 'I'm not used to being afraid,' I said, but all the same I was afraid. 'We only brought you here,' the female said, 'because we hope that you may be interested. We are rather in need of a dashing young associate at the moment and we wondered whether we might persuade you to become it.' 'Oh,' I said, 'what are you: a gang of crooks?' 'Oh no,' she said, 'a business community.' 'Oh,' I said, 'what business does your community do?' 'Social service,' she said, 'setting straight injustices with the least possible inconvenience to all concerned.' 'And how do you do it?' I asked. 'You would soon learn if you would join us. It's an interesting world for our younger agents: lots of motorcars, lots of aeroplanes. Life is one long, gay social whirl.' 'And what is the work?' I asked. 'Ah,' she said, 'we shall discuss that if you express a willingness to become one of us.' 'If your job were honest,' I said, 'you'd say what it is. It can't be nice or it wouldn't have you in it.' 'If children are pert here,' she said, 'we make them into dog biscuit.' So I said, 'If ladies are pert to me I make them into cat's meat.'

"We should have become quite eloquent, but a man's face appeared at the bars and he said, 'Now, ladies, ladies, the first word in business of any kind is unity. Do let us have unity. Without that we can never get anywhere. Now, Miss Jones, if we cannot have unity from you, let us have some information. When Mr Cole Hawlings gave his performance of Punch and Judy at Seekings, did he hand you a small black Box?' 'No,' I said, 'he didn't.' 'Did he leave it with one of the others of your party there, or hide it in Seekings House?' 'How on earth should I know?' I said. 'That's the point,' he answered. 'Do you know?' 'No, I don't know,' I said.

" 'If I were you, sir,' the woman said, 'I would put this young person into the scrounger. D'you know what a scrounger is, my

[79]

dear? It has a thing in it that goes round and round and round and then presently, of course, the thing scrounged becomes dog biscuit.' At that the shutter went across the bars and the light went out. I was in absolute darkness and utter silence. I don't know how long I was in that absolute blackness when suddenly, down came something thick and warm and woolly right over my head and shoulders and that horrible woman's voice said, 'All right, you needn't kick, I only want to know if you've got this Box on you.'

"Well, I was searched and then I was carried back along the little passage and put into the taxi which had brought me. They turned on a little light in the taxi roof and I saw they had put me a pot of tea and some cold ham and some bread inside the taxi, so I made a hearty meal. I waited and waited for what seemed like hours. I didn't hear any sound of men, only from time to time I thought I heard, very, very far away, the noise of water falling, quite a lot of water, a sort of waterfall. Then the light went out and I was in the dark. The next thing I knew, the taxi was moving and then we gave that sort of lurching leap as an aeroplane does and we were away in the air, going higher and higher and making no noise. Then we were on the ground, running along the road. We stopped, the bottom of the aeroplane quietly opened and dropped me through it and before I could get onto my feet it had moved away. There I was in the churchyard, with the Condicote church clock striking nine and chiming, and the taxi or aeroplane, or whatever it was, was away."

"I say," Peter said, "you do have all the luck."

"Come along down to the larder," Kay said. "Jemima, you might put on a kettle and we'll boil her up some cocoa."

"I'm not going to drink any poison like cocoa, thank you," Maria said. "When one's had a nervous strain such as I have, one wants a posset with three fresh eggs in it and a spoonful of sherry." They went into the larder and found a nourishing meal after Maria's own heart. Then Jemima and Susan took her up to bed and gave her a posset.

Kay and Peter went up to their rooms. "Well, I'm blessed," Peter said, "we are having a holiday. I wonder what was in the black Box that the gang wanted?"

"I hope they won't kidnap any more of us," Kay said, and with that he slipped the black Box under his pyjama coat next to his skin, rolled over and fell asleep.

He hadn't been long asleep before he woke in a state of perplexity and excitement. He kept thinking of what Maria had told him. She might have been fifty feet under the ground, in cold stone walls and cold stone floors, he thought. And where was it I heard about caves underneath the ground? It was that Roman chap last night, talking about Chester Hills. He said, "It's a limestone country, all honeycombed with caves and those Wolves, as we call them, were all underground." I wonder whether this gang is at Chester Hills? What if this Theological Missionary College should really be a gang in disguise? I do wish my guardian were here and I could ask her advice.

Then he slept again and seemed to hear the voice of Caroline Louisa calling to him in great distress from a great distance and it seemed that he asked, "Where are you?" and heard her cry, "Here," and ran towards the voice and found nothing but stone walls against which he beat and thrust, but could find no door nor any window. But through the thickness of the stone came the voice, "I'm shut up here in the darkness, Kay. I don't know where it is, but it's somewhere where I can hear the noise of water falling."

When he woke again it was time to get up, so he dressed and was down by eight o'clock. By some fortune or freak the post was in, in spite of the Christmas rush, but as Ellen said, it was probably the post of two days before.

There was no letter from Caroline Louisa.

CHAPTER EIGHT

WHILE HE was looking through the letters next morning Ellen brought him the paper. "Oh, Master Kay," she said, "have you heard the news? The Bishop of Tatchester has disappeared."

"What?" Kay said.

"The papers are full of it," Ellen said. "The reverend gentleman went out of the Palace last night for a brisk walk before going to bed, according to his custom, and he hasn't come back." Kay opened the paper.

STARTLING DISAPPEARANCE OF THE BISHOP OF TATCHESTER

Considerable alarm was caused in ecclesiastical circles last night when it was known that His Grace, the Bishop of Tatchester, had failed to return to the Palace and was not heard of at the time of our going to press. The very reverend gentleman had passed the evening at the Palace in making ready for the Christmas season and in despatching his Christmas cards to the clergy of his Diocese, a duty that His Grace leaves to no hands but his own. On conclusion of this pleasant duty His Grace signified to his sister, Dame Eleanor Chasuble, that he would go for a brisk walk through the precincts before retiring to rest. According to her nightly custom Dame Chasuble prepared tea for His Grace on his return. At midnight when he had not returned she became alarmed and telephoned to the Dean, who enquired at once of the hospital if His Grace had been the victim of an accident, but receiving a negative response they communicated with the Police and although an active search was at once instituted we regret to announce that no news has been received of His Grace's whereabouts. It will be remembered that the Palace was the scene of a serious burglary the night before last and it is thought that the Bishop's disappearance may be connected with the earlier outrage. We are sure that we voice the feelings of thousands of our readers when we extend to Dame Chasuble our heartiest sympathy in her anxiety and our liveliest hopes that His Grace may soon be restored to the bosom of his household and his Diocese.

"I say," Kay said to himself, "now they've got the Bishop. It's the same gang after this Box of Delights, and they think the Bishop's got it."

While he was meditating this in the dining-room Peter came down.

"You look pretty gloomy, Kay," Peter said.

"I am pretty gloomy," Kay said. "They've scrobbled the Bishop."

"And who d'you think they are?" Peter said.

"I know you think it's absurd, Peter, but I think they're the Missionary College people out at Chester Hills. Would you come with me to see what kind of place it is?"

"I don't mind," Peter said. "Shall we go after breakfast?"

"I was thinking we might get there and back before breakfast," Kay said, leading the way to the door.

"How on earth could we get about forty miles and back?" Peter said.

Kay caught hold of his arm and with his other hand twitched the button on the magic Box. Instantly both of them were plucked through the air so swiftly that they saw the fields and brooks in a kind of blur beneath them. Then suddenly they were whirled downwards and there they were on a hillside, standing on what was the rampart of an old camp, both a little out of breath.

"Now, this is Chester Hills," Kay said, "and that's Hope-under-Chesters where the curates got in who I believe picked my pocket. You can see this was once a Roman camp, too."

"Where do you want to go now?" Peter said.

"I think down there, into that valley," Kay said.

Looking down on the valley the boys saw nothing but a great woodland which began a little way below the camp and filled all the valley, but there were folds in it and what there was in the folds they could not see.

"You can see from the lie of the land," said Kay, "that a road ran out of this gateway down the hill. I'll bet if you had a spade to clear away the turf you'd come upon a Roman pavement underneath."

He led the way down the hill and presently the lines of the Roman track became more difficult to follow. When they came to the edge of the wood the track was barred by a locked and chained gate. There was a notice nailed to a tree:

TRESPASSERS WILL BE PROSECUTED

and on another tree there was a bigger notice:

DANGER!
MAN-TRAPS AND SPRING-GUNS

The track inside the wood was hardly more than a woodland
path. The wood, which contained a great deal of yew and other
dark evergreens, looked curiously forbidding and evil and in
the darkness and wetness, with its profuse mass of close,
sinister growth, it put a chill on both boys' hearts.

"It doesn't look a very cheery place," Peter said. "I don't
think we ought to risk those notices."

"Oh rats!" Kay said. "I don't believe in any of those notices.
For years I was scared of a notice that said, 'Bloodhounds', and
there wasn't a bloodhound in the county. Come along in, but
we'd better not talk much and we won't make more noise than
we must."

He clambered over the gate and Peter followed him along the
woodland track, which led downhill. As it bent and twisted
Kay went forward boldly but Peter went with a beating heart.

"I say, Kay," Peter said, "I wish you wouldn't hurry on like
this. You ought to go cautiously."

"It's absolutely safe," Kay said, "do look, nobody's been on
this woodland track for weeks."

"But a keeper might come at any minute," Peter said.

"There aren't keepers," Kay said. "You can see that this
place isn't preserved or we'd have seen pheasants long ago or
keepers' vermin boards or dead stoats and weasels and poor,
beautiful owls."

Presently they passed from the woodland to a rather denser
part that was more like a neglected shrubbery with azaleas and
rhododendrons, all straggled and overgrown. Between lines of
box trees, however, a path that seemed to be in considerable
use led to right and left and through gaps in the dense
shrubbery the boys saw the gleam of water just below them.

"Let's go on down and look at the water," said Kay.

They left the path and thrust through the shrubbery where it seemed thinnest until they were just inside a rhododendron bush on the very lip of the water which stretched before them in a very long and beautiful lake. It was not much more than a hundred yards across but it gave Kay the illusion of great depth and of being very evil, dark as it was, fringed on both sides by beautiful trees, nearly all dark.

"I say," Kay said, "what a place!"

"It gives me the fantods," Peter answered. "I don't like this place."

"Well, we've come here now," Kay said. "Do let's examine it before we go."

Away to the left the lake came to an end in some tumbled rocks and boulders beyond which the ground rose, with shrubberies and ornamental trees and beyond the trees, buildings seemingly of great extent. They were yellowish, Kay thought, as though built of Cotswold stone, and from somewhere within their mass a little bell chimed gracefully for the half hour.

"Now I'm going along here to look at the house," Kay said. "You coming?"

"No, I don't think I will, thanks," Peter said. "You go and have a look at the house if you like. I'll just go along and look at the boat-house and see if one could come here in the summer for a swim."

"Well, do look out for yourself," Kay said. "That little clock has just chimed for half-past eight. When it chimes for nine you be inside the track we came by. You can easily take cover and wait for me."

He went off along the path between the box trees and he hadn't gone very far before he heard footsteps and voices coming towards him. One was the unmistakable, high voice of the foxy-faced man, saying, "So you'll get them all in the soup, ha-ha, what?"

Something followed which Kay could not quite catch, but the next voice was undoubtedly that of Abner.

"As to that matter, sir," Abner was saying in his silky-soft voice, "that's a question that must wait until we've had our bathe and our breakfast. Perhaps they will be in a better mood and more disposed to be reasonable after their good night's rest."

The men passed where Kay was hidden without seeing him. The foxy-faced man said, "It will be mighty cold. One plunge and then out will be enough for me."

"It will be exhilarating," Abner said.

Kay heard feet running upon springboards and two splashes, followed by splutterings. The foxy-faced man was saying, "It's like iced water, what?"

Kay heard them crawling up the steps from the water and Abner saying, "Enough for honour. We will leave the rest to the British."

He heard them rubbing themselves down and muttering with clacking teeth that their blood would never run warm again. Soon they had their robes round them and were running back along the path by which they had come.

Kay went out from his hiding-place and crept along in the direction in which they had gone. Presently he came to the end of the lake among the tumbled rocks and boulders. At first he could see no outlet to the water but then heard, among the sighing of the pine trees, a sort of wash of water. The path by which the bathers had come led above the tumble of rock. He followed it through a dense shrubbery and presently came into a thicket of laurel bordering on a drive. Through the laurel he could see a spacious mansion, built in Cotswold stone somewhere early in the reign of George the Third, on a foundation much older. He was looking directly across at great double front doors within a portico. They were lofty doors paned with glass to give light to the hall within and while he watched there came from within the house the sweet banging of a gong. Almost immediately half a dozen men wearing black cloaks came out of the outhouses to the right of the house and passed through the front doors.

Just as the last of them passed under the portico there came a loud hissing noise, something between a whistle and an escape of steam from somewhere up in the air. A laurel was rather in the way, but Kay saw the men in black look up towards the noise and looked up himself. To his amazement he saw a silvery aeroplane poised just like a kestrel above the house, hovering in a way that Kay hadn't thought possible, and the whistle or hiss of steam was plainly a signal for a moment later the aeroplane sank slowly down vertically, as though into the very body of the house.

'Whoever would have thought an aeroplane could do that!' thought Kay. 'I suppose that's the kind of aeroplane that scrobbled Maria. Now, I wonder if poor old Cole Hawlings and the Bishop and perhaps Caroline Louisa are shut up in dungeons only a few yards away?'

However, it was now time to start back towards Peter. As he crossed above the tumbled rocks he looked again, hoping to see some opening among them. This time he saw what he ought to have noticed before, a sluice with its winch, beside which was a rusty iron grating, so covered with drift of different sorts that it could not easily be distinguished.

At this moment the bell above the Missionary College struck nine and chimed the hour. Kay hurried to the place where Peter was to be, but Peter was not there.

'Oh, where has he gone?' he thought. 'What should I have done if I had been in Peter's place?'

He followed along the path by which he thought Peter might have gone on an exploration. A little brook ran across the path and in the mud by the brook's bank was the mark of Peter's shoes. Presently the ground began to be very soft, with a good many springs breaking out. Here Peter's tracks were plain indeed. On the farther side of the soft patch the track turned a corner and there, to Kay's horror, were other tracks. Two or three men had been there and there were little fresh, unmistakable signs of rapid trampling and scuffling. 'There's no doubt about it,' Kay thought, 'they've scrobbled Peter.'

He reckoned up the chances and decided that it would be safe to follow after these people, whoever they were, but he had not gone far before he heard the noise of oars on the lake. Peering through the branches he saw, pulling towards the mansion on the far side, a boat in whose stern sheets lay something that looked like a roll of blanket. 'That's Peter, scrobbled,' Kay thought. 'I'll get back home and speak to the Inspector and perhaps by that time there will be a word from Caroline Louisa.'

He took up his Box of Delights and pressed the knob. A sort of whirlwind plucked him up between the treetops and snatched him to the box-tree walk at Seekings, where he was set gently upon his feet.

He found the other children at breakfast. "You're very late, Kay," Maria said. "Have you seen the latest? Here." She unfolded the paper for him:

MYSTERIOUS DISAPPEARANCE
OF THE MERRY DEAN

Ecclesiastical and other circles have been convulsed at Tatchester by the strange disappearance of the well-known Dean from the precincts. It appears that the Dean went out shortly after dark last night, in response to what was said to have been an urgent summons, and has not yet been heard of.

It is feared at the Deanery that he has been the victim of a motorcar accident but we are entitled to our own conviction that the disappearance of the reverend gentleman, coming so soon after the burglary at the Palace and the disappearance of His Grace the Bishop, are crimes perpetrated by some local gang. Something like a reign of terror exists at this moment throughout Tatchester.

It is hardly necessary to remind our readers that the Dean of Tatchester is the well-known author of *Possible Oriental Influences in Ancient Philosophies*, as well as the famous handbook, *Cheerfulness: the Christian Duty*.

"Now, what do you think of that?" Maria said. "That's the gang that scrobbled me."

"I believe they've scrobbled Peter, too," Kay said, "and as soon as I've had some breakfast I'll go round to the police station."

"I love to see sleuths at work," Maria said, "so I'll come too." They went round and the Inspector welcomed them.

"Come in, Miss Maria and Master Kay," he said. "What is it now? More clues for the Law to follow?" Kay told his story and all his suspicions.

"Ha," the Inspector said. "And footprints in the mud, you say, and the roll of blanket in the boat. But you're quite wrong, Master Kay, in saying that the Principal of the Training College is a Mr Brown. It's Father Boddledale, as I told you. I'll telephone him now."

He telephoned: "Is that you, Your Reverence?" he asked. "I'm the Inspector of Police speaking. I want to ask you if you have seen anything of a lad aged ten, by the name of Peter, who was out at your place this morning . . . You haven't seen him? . . . Hasn't been seen at all? . . . Thank you. And have you with you a gentleman by the name of Abner Brown? . . . No? . . . Well, you will forgive my disturbing you at your good work . . . Thank you, sir, and I wish the same to you.

"You see, Master Kay," he said, hanging up the telephone, "they know nothing of Master Peter there, but it's my belief about boys that 'leave them alone and they'll come home'."

Kay thanked him and they returned home. "Pompous old ass," Maria said.

"He's a jolly good chap really," Kay said. "He mayn't be quite a Sherlock Holmes but he's most awfully good about rabbits."

As they went into the little street, more newsboys came rushing from the station shouting, "Special edition of the *Tatchester Times*!" "Another disappearance – Special!" "Canons of Tatchester disappear – Special!"

Kay bought a paper, for which the boy charged him sixpence. He read the little sheet, which was still wet from the press:

We feel that this morning's events are so extraordinary that we are warranted in making them the subject of a special edition of our paper.

The night before last our deservedly popular Prelate was torn from us; last night the World's Dean, as we may call him, similarly disappeared; early this morning, while they were walking back from the early morning service, Canon Honeytongue and Canon Balmblossom, his friend, were met by a messenger who told them that the Dean had met with a motor accident, was suffering from a slight concussion and was asking eagerly to see them. The reverend gentlemen then hurried to the waiting car and on asking the driver how long they would be, were told, 'Less than an hour'. They called to their friends, others of the Cathedral Clergy who were accompanying them through the Close, that they would be back to breakfast. The anxiety of the people of Tatchester may be judged when the breakfast hour passed without any message whatsoever from the missing Canons.

We ask all the inhabitants of the Diocese to come forward at once in aiding the Police by reporting the movements of all cars likely to have been concerned in the removal of the reverend gentlemen. The car is reported to have been a large black, dark blue, dark brown or even dark green or grey saloon, with a clean-shaven driver in a dark suit. Anyone who may have seen such a car in any of the country roads in the hours between five and seven-thirty this morning is asked to telephone at once to the Chief of Tatchester Constabulary: telephone number Tatchester 7000.

In the meantime we convey to all the members of the Cathedral Establishment our heart-felt sympathy with their anxiety.

"Now what d'you think of that?" Maria said.

"Wait a moment," Kay said, "there's some Stop Press news here at the side:

STOP PRESS NEWS

The rumour current that the missing Prelate was seen near Chester Hills last night turns out to be without foundation. The gentleman mistaken for the Bishop was the Reverend Father Boddledale of the Ecclesiastical Training College, who has long been known as the Bishop's double. No reliable information has reached the Authorities about any of the missing dignitaries.

"I know what I think of it," Kay said. "They've got the Bishop, the Dean, the Punch and Judy man, the two Canons and Peter in that den of theirs at Chester Hills."

"If I were you, I'd telephone the Yard," Maria said. "It's no good going to your champion rabbit man or whatever he is: go to the sleuths whose job it is to sleuth."

They telephoned the Yard, who referred them to the Chief of the Tatchester Constabulary: telephone number Tatchester 7000. When they rang the number they were told that the matter would meet with every attention and although no news had come about any of the missing gentlemen they expected developments before the evening.

At lunchtime Kay was called to the telephone. Caroline Louisa's sister wanted to speak about her brother who was now better. Kay explained that Caroline Louisa had not returned from London and had left no word.

"Well," the sister said, "she set off from here two days ago. Whatever can have happened?"

Kay had a shrewd suspicion what had happened and went back to lunch feeling very miserable. After lunch it came on to rain, there was still no news of Peter and it wasn't possible to play in the garden. He went upstairs to his room, locked the doors, covered the keyholes as before, ducked under the valance of the dressing-table and looked again into the Box of Delights.

This time he looked into an entirely different scene. There was a little hill with a beech clump upon it and a vixen playing with her cubs on some tumbled chalk outside a barrow. A badger was padding about; from the glow upon the wood it seemed to Kay to be about sunset on a fine May evening, but presently he was aware that some of the glow upon the trees was due to the presence of multitudes of butterflies – painted ladies, red admirals, peacocks, purple emperors, chalk blues, commas, tortoiseshells, purple and green hairstreaks, and others – Camberwell beauties and swallowtails – and all these began moving suddenly towards him. He noticed that they were drawing an airy chariot made out of rose leaves from some sweetbriar rose. Although it looked very fragile, Kay stepped into the chariot and at once the butterflies lifted him up high over the treetops, going much more swiftly than he would have thought possible and although their flight wavered now up, now down, it was extraordinarily delightful.

Soon they were flying over the very wood from which Peter had disappeared, but inside the wood and all round the great house, as Kay drew near it, there were Wolves running and snarling with their hackles up and teeth gleaming. He had never thought it possible that there could be so many.

Then, at one little window, as Kay floated past, he saw Caroline Louisa stretching out her hands to him, calling, "Help me, Kay!" Instantly two great she-Wolves dragged her from the window and pulled down an iron shutter.

The butterflies changed their direction and flew away and away from Chester Hills, and at last brought Kay to a bare mountain which he had never before seen. In the mountainside there was a little door with a knocker. Kay knocked at the knocker and a little old man opened the door and said, "Will you please to walk in, Master Kay? And what would you like to see: the treasures or the work?"

"I should like to see both, please," Kay said.

The little old man opened a door and there was a furnace with bellows and an anvil, with other little men hard at work making extraordinary things out of metals and precious stones. Kay was so delighted that he stared and stared and at last one of them plucked a piece of gold, beat it rapidly into the shape of a little rosebud and thrust it into Kay's buttonhole. Then the little old man said that it would be time for him to be going and led him to the stone door on the hillside where there was a sort of boat harnessed to wild duck.

When he got into the boat the wild duck flew with it high into the air over the dark woods, and then down and down and down, till at last he was just over Seekings House and had only to drop down the chimney, as it seemed, into his room. Just as he snapped the Box to in his pocket there came a clattering at the door.

"Kay! Kay!" Maria cried.

"What is it?" Kay said.

"What isn't it?" she said. "They've got the whole of the Cathedral staff." In the study she showed him a paper. There was a single sheet, still damp from the press, the big black headings easily smudged:

And there was a note:

> We had thought that the mystery attached to the disappearance of the eminent Clergy of the Tatchester Establishment would by this time have been cleared up. We regret to say that our confidence was gravely misplaced. Tonight we have to report the complete disappearance of the Precentor, the Vesturer, the Bursar, the Canons Minor, the Archdeacon, Vergers, Organist and, it is feared, other members of the Cathedral staff.
>
> Anyone able to throw the slightest light on this very dark mystery are adjured to communicate at once with the local Police (telephone Tatchester 7000) and to spare no pains in bringing the offenders to justice.

"We've been wondering where on earth you've been," Maria said.

"Oh," Kay said, "I suppose I fell asleep."

"What a very pretty shiny buttonhole you've got," Maria said. "What is it?"

"Just a little rose," Kay said looking down, and indeed there in his buttonhole was the golden rose that had been made for him in the mountain.

They waited up until the news on the wireless and heard that the Archbishops were determined that in case of need the services should be held in the Cathedral in spite of the absence of the regular staff and that certain clergy had been asked to proceed to Tatchester to officiate there if the need arose. The announcer said that the matter was viewed with the greatest seriousness and that the public was asked to cooperate with the Police by giving instant, accurate information of a red, white, blue, grey, brown or black motor-bus – the colours had been variously given by various observers – proceeding at a frightening pace in the direction of Tatchester some twenty minutes before the alleged outrage.

"I say!" Kay said. "There'll be a fine old twitter in Tatchester."

"Well," Maria said, "if they survive they'll have something to talk of as long as they live. Next to being martyred I should think being scrobbled would be the greatest joy a clergyman could have. I should prefer it to being martyred myself, but tastes differ."

With that she went to put some holly in Jemima's bed and then retired to rest.

CHAPTER NINE

KAY WENT back to his room sorely perplexed. It was time for
bed, but the sight of Peter's bed without Peter reminded him
that the Wolves were Running: he could not think of sleeping.
'Oh, if I could only find out where Cole Hawlings is,' he
thought, 'then I could give him back his Box and put an end to
all this kidnapping.'

He stayed looking at the fire without any thought of undres-
sing. At last, in his misery, he opened the Box, thinking,
"Perhaps I may see Herne the Hunter. He might be able to give
me some advice."

When he opened the Box it seemed to him that he passed
through a stone gateway to the waters of a lake where a boatman
sat in a little green boat.

Kay stepped into the boat, the boatman thrust her off and

rowed her over the lake, which was so clear that Kay could see the golden and scarlet fishes on the pebbles at the bottom.

Kay landed at the other side of the lake and walked up an avenue of fruit trees at the end of which was a Castle. Out of the Castle to meet him came the Lady of the Oak Tree, still wearing the ring with the longways cross. She seemed to be about twenty now and more beautiful, Kay thought, than even Caroline Louisa.

"Ah, Kay," she said, "I know why you've come to me today. You will hear more tomorrow if you go to Chester Hills. Now that you are here, what of all things would you like to see?"

"Well, of all things," he said, "a tournament."

At once he was looking into the courtyard of the Castle, which was now divided into two by a gaily-painted barrier. The sides of the yard were lined with tiers of seats, full of people and gay with banners.

At each end of the lists two Knights, one in scarlet, one in white armour, were taking position on horses excited by the music and the crowd. Suddenly the trumpeters in the Royal Box blew all together, the Knights dropped their lances to the rests, drove in their spurs and hurtled at each other on different sides of the barrier. Under the Royal Box they struck each other's shields with their spears; they themselves reeled in their saddles but were not unseated, the spears broke at the guards and leaped a dozen feet into the air. The Knights finished their courses, then wheeled round and waited for fresh spears.

"Would you like to do that, Kay?" the Lady asked.

"Oh, I would," he said.

A squire led forth a war-horse with blue and white trappings and out of the wall the pieces of a suit of armour walked towards him and buckled themselves about him, first the foot gear, leggings and cuisses, then the body-armour and arm-pieces, lastly the helmet with its plume. A squire came forward to give him a leg-up into the saddle and another brought him a lance.

"It is not always wise to take part in the Past, Kay," the Lady said. "Arnold of Todi did so, as you may hear tomorrow, and where in the Past is he now? He is lost, Kay."

But Kay could not think of Arnold of Todi; he was on a great horse, feeling its mouth and staring through the slit of his helmet at his enemy at the other end. His enemy was a Red Knight, just gathering his shield which he now turned to Kay so that he saw upon it a black wolf rampant. A squire handed him a white shield with blue chevrons on it, but before he could take it the trumpets blew. At once he drove forward at the Wolf Knight. The horses whinnied, the joy of the charge surged up in him, he saw the red helm crouched above the Wolf. Then, crash, they met.

"I've got him," Kay shouted, as he felt his spear drive home onto the Red Knight's chest and the Knight go backward over the crupper.

He *had* got him, but something odd had happened to himself. "My girths are gone," he cried. He felt the saddle turn under his horse's belly while he was flung headlong, endlong, anylong down, down, down, back to his room at Seekings.

Next morning, as soon as ever it was light, he dressed. Taking the Box he turned the knob first so that he might become tiny, next so that he might go swiftly, and instantly he was whirled up through the chimney, out through the cowl and away, just as it was growing light. He felt so minute that he trembled lest a sparrow should peck him in mistake for a caterpillar. In a moment he was whirled down to the doorstep of the great house at Chester Hills, still clutching the Box. He was shrunken to the size of one of his leaden soldiers. The front door was open and he was on the top step: he walked towards the hall.

There came the pad of straw-soled slippers on the stone corridor and Kay could see the end of a dark green apron, also the head of a broom which the old man was trailing after him.

The broom began its work under the window-seat. In one instant it was rushing at Kay with a row of bristling hairs like a small plantation, which swept him off his feet. Kay was rolled over and over into the open hall, with his eyes tight shut for fear of being blinded and clutching the Box of Delights lest he should lose it.

He picked himself up and contrived to press the knob on the Box, saying, "I want to go fast to the chief room in this place."

Instantly he was plucked through the wall, along a corridor into a room where he was set down on a shelf of books, six feet from the floor. He heard the bell of the house chime for half-past eight. Then a pleasant, silky voice came towards him from along the passage, singing a popular song.

"That's Abner Brown," Kay muttered, "and he wouldn't sing unless he were doing something pretty bad."

Kay slipped in between two of the English poets as Abner entered the room.

"What news? What news?" Abner muttered.

He pressed the button of a bell and sat at his desk. Presently someone entered.

"Did you please to ring, oh Father?" the newcomer asked.

"Yes, Nineteen," Abner said, "I did ring. "Send Seven here, will you please?"

Presently a robust voice was heard approaching from the back of the house. It was singing a song which was certainly not the song for a young clergyman:

> "A rum-rum-tiddly-um,
> Who'll have a drink with me?"

The door was shoved open and a man came striding in. He was the big man called Joe whom Kay had seen at the Rupert's Arms. He was laughing and singing in a breath.

"You want me, Chief?" he said.

"You might close the door, perhaps," Abner said. "Gently."

The man, from where he stood, made a long leg and kicked the door to. Then he drew near to Abner's desk and stood there waiting.

"I hear you've permitted yourself some little criticisms of my orders about these clergymen," Abner said.

Kay saw at once that Joe was asking himself, "Who on earth could have told him that?"

"Odd how the news gets about here, isn't it?" Abner said.

"You're right," Joe said.

"So you *have* been criticising my orders. Why?"

"If I knew why the orders were given," said Joe, "I might see sense in them, but to kidnap a lot of clergymen who can't afford any ransom worth your while seems to me a lot of foolishness. You've roused the Press, you've roused the Yard and you've roused the Nation . . . All to get a Box, you say, that belongs to the Punch and Judy man."

"Correct," Abner said. "That was in the possession of the Punch and Judy man would be better, perhaps."

"That's why we criticise," Joe said. "You know that this old man, Cole Hawlings, had the Box when he went to Seekings House and hadn't got it next morning. Well, you've got him, haven't you? What we can't understand is why you don't make him tell you where he put it."

"How would you make him?" Abner asked.

"He's an old man, a bit of a talking-to would make him tell. No need to hurt him: threaten him with a red-hot poker or keep him awake with Itchy Powder. If he'd scratched all these last two nights he'd have told you by this time."

"Then you don't realise who Cole Hawlings is? Did you ever hear of Ramon Lully?"

"You mean the chap who did the box trick at the Coliseum?" Joe asked.

"No, Joe, not the Coliseum man," Abner said. "The man I mean was a philosopher of the Middle Ages whose tomb they show at Palma. Remember the name, for I shall allude to it later. Did you ever hear of Arnold of Todi?"

"No, I can't say I ever did," Joe said. "What was he, or is he?"

"He too was a philosopher of the Middle Ages," said Abner, "and not really very much is known of him. But the son of one of his disciples left some papers which say that he and Lully were rivals. Lully was all for finding an Elixir of Life that would make him last through the Future. Arnold was always trying to find some power of entering the Past."

"Golly!" Joe said. "They were a couple of queer coughdrops, if you ask me."

"I'm not asking you," Abner said, "I'm telling you. This unknown man whom I mentioned says in his papers that Arnold, by some extraordinary magic power, created a Box, by means of which he could enter the Past at will."

"In fact he did the box trick," said Joe, "like that chap at the Coliseum."

"Now," Abner said, "some think that Arnold entered the Past by means of this Box and could not get out of it but is wandering there for ever. Anyhow, he disappeared, but the Box, the man says, remained and came at last into the hands of a lady who was afraid of it. She kept it in Stiborough Castle about twenty miles from here and when Stiborough was besieged in the Civil War she buried the Box in the castle-vaults. This woman, Aurelia Stiborough, when she was old repented of her folly. She wrote down the bearings of the hiding-place in cipher. But perhaps, my dear Joe, I worry you with this. I should be desolated to inflict boredom on an old friend."

"Go ahead," Joe said, "now we've begun I may as well know it all."

"Well, we came here," Abner said. "I have always been interested in magic, as you know. For many years I have been aware of all the stories about Arnold of Todi, but like most students of magic I believe that the Box must have fallen into the hands of the Inquisitors or Puritans and been burned.

"I have always been interested in ciphers of different kinds and quite by accident came upon this Stiborough cipher whilst I was stopping with the Bishop at the time of the Missionary Conference. Well, a cipher will always yield its secrets if you go on long enough and this one gave way to me, although it was a very ingenious thing.

"You're not an imaginative man, Joe, but you can imagine my excitement at finding that this amazing treasure of one of the amazing men of all time was buried in the earth less than twenty miles from here."

"So then, I suppose, you got busy," Joe said.

"Busy!" Abner said. "You little know what I went through. I learned what the cipher contained at two in the morning here. Before three I was on the site of Stiborough Castle: pitch-dark night, gale blowing, rain coming down in torrents, ivy blowing loose from the wall, bits of boughs flying everywhere, the Castle in such a mess of old broken stones and earth and bramble that I almost broke my neck half a dozen times. And then, Joe, I made my measurements. I was wet through, cold to the marrow, but I didn't mind wet, I didn't mind cold. And there, by the first rays of light, I saw that I was too late: someone had read the cipher a little before me. There were the brambles cut away and the shaft sunk in exactly the right place and at the bottom of the pit the marks showed that I was too late."

"Gee!" Joe said with feeling. "It isn't often you're too late."

"Well, there it was. The Box had gone but it hadn't been gone long and the next question was to get it from the man who had it. Who had it? Who'd been digging at Stiborough and making enquiries there? The only man who had been near the ruins was a little old man who played a Punch and Judy show."

"Cole Hawlings," Joe said. "Well, you've got him all right, you've no cause to complain. I suppose it wasn't hard to run him down – an old man with a Punch and Judy show?"

"By certain magical ways I was able to find out who Cole Hawlings really is. When you see your friends again you will be able to tell them why I have never hurt him. Cole Hawlings is Ramon Lully."

Kay saw Joe gasp and then assume a look of pity, contempt and tolerance for a man plainly gone mad.

"But you said he was dead, Chief," Joe said at last.

"I said, 'They show his tomb at Palma'. He discovered the Elixir of Life and flew away from his disciples in the likeness of a golden cock and here he is now as Cole Hawlings."

"That thing you say he discovered, the liquor of life and that, would be a kind of cough mixture?"

"If you can imagine a cough mixture that will make a man eternal, able to survive pestilence or any other way of death . . ."

"It would be a good mixture to get on the market, I can see," Joe said. "These patent medicines just rake in the money. And should we all be in it with you?"

"My dear Joe," Abner said, "if there is one thing I pride myself on it is my loyalty to my colleagues. For whom do I toil here? For whom do I think and worry and scheme, but for the Brotherhood? We have lived through all these years of danger and adventure together. What could be a greater joy to me than to share all our little takings and to enter into partnership for the marketing of an Elixir, for an eternity of happy quiet?"

"About these clergymen," Joe said, "what we still don't see is why you keep scrobbling the clergymen. See here now in *The Daily Thriller*:

The latest outrage at Tatchester points to the existence of an organised conspiracy, possibly, as has been suggested, to prevent the holding of the Millennial Christmas Service advertised for the early hours of Christmas morning. We would warn the scoundrels responsible that the Establishment will contrive to defeat their machinations.

THE SERVICE WILL BE HELD.

You see that, Chief, and the heading 'Church Defies Bandits'. They mean business."

"So do I, Joe," Abner said.

"Is it your game to stop that Service?" Joe asked.

"I'll stop that Service if they don't deliver the Box or tell me where it is."

Kay saw looks of anger, bewilderment, contempt and mutiny cross Joe's face in quick succession. He noticed too that none of these looks was missed by Abner, who was watching Joe intently. Joe rose from his chair and walked the room for a moment.

"Chief," Joe said, "I don't like what you're doing. While you were just a fair-and-square burglar like the rest of us I respected you, but this dabbling in magic and scrobbling up the clergy will come to no good. You'll find it so when it's too late. The Press respects burglars like us who only burgle the very rich, but you're going now against children, women and the Clergy and you've turned the Press dead against you. Of course I've got no intellect, don't go by what I say . . ."

"Come to the point. What is it?" Abner asked.

"Well, Chief," Joe said, "now would be the time to stop this clergy business. The Archbishop is offering a reward of a thousand pounds for the return of the Bishop or Dean, with reduced sums for the rest. It's twenty-five quid even for a choir-boy. It would be quite a profitable little haul if you chose to take it. Tomorrow, or even today, you'll have the Yard poking about."

"The Yard! The Yard could be in this room and those clergy could shout 'O Come, all ye Faithful!' at the tops of their voices and not be heard. Come to breakfast."

"All right," Joe said, "but there is another thing. There is a boy at Seekings: Kay Harker. He was there with that boy Peter who we scrobbled and I don't see why Cole Hawlings shouldn't have given the Box to him if it comes to that."

"You don't see a good many things," Abner said.

[105]

"I daresay I'm as blind as a bat," Joe said, "and as for intellect, I never claimed any, but blind and barmy as I am I never talked such tosh as you've talked since I came into this room, nor I never sold my soul to the devil. You've got bats in your belfry. I thought so before and now I know it. You'll come to a bad end, let me tell you, and it won't be long hence . . ."

Kay saw Abner's pale face turn a little whiter. He was plainly very angry and about to answer savagely when the door opened and in came Sylvia Daisy Pouncer Brown, who had no doubt been listening at the keyhole. On seeing her, Joe muttered what sounded like, "Crikey, now here's his Missus." Sylvia D. P. Brown looked at Joe and drew her own conclusions.

"Abner my dear," she said, "you've talked and talked. Do come to breakfast before it's all cold. Remember, you've got to speak a Christmas talk at Tatchester Alms Houses at half-past ten."

"I was forgetting the Alms Houses," Abner said. "Those poor deserving old men and women, we mustn't forget them, must we? Well, Joe, that will delay our business till half-past two, in my room. Do you get that?"

"Half-past two, in your room. Very well, Chief," said Joe.

They walked out of the room together.

'I'll come back at half-past two,' thought Kay, 'and hear what those two are up to.'

He turned the knob of the Box so that he might go swiftly. At once he was borne away on unseen wings back to his late breakfast at Seekings, with the three girls, each sure that Peter would be all right and all thrilled at the disappearance of every single clergyman attached to the Cathedral.

"The gang has put the clergy's backs up now," Susan said. "You see what the Archbishops say: 'They are happy to state that five clergy from the Diocese have proceeded to Tatchester to provide the Christmas Services if by any unhappy occurrence the rightful Ministers be unable to officiate'."

"They ought not to have mentioned that," Maria said. "Now

the gang will scrobble those too, you'll see."

Kay did not answer this. He was thinking how very powerful the gang was and how miserable the beautiful Caroline Louisa must be, shut up in the rock with two women like she-wolves as guards.

After breakfast he went round to the Inspector.

"If you please," Kay said, "would you like to win the Archbishop's reward of a thousand pounds? If you would go to the Tatchester Barracks and fall out the Tatshire Blues and raid the Chester Hills College you'd find the clergy there, I'm sure you would."

"Why, how you run on about the College, Master Kay," the Inspector said. "This is what in Medical Circles is spoken of as a Hobsession. No, no, believe me, the College is all full of young Reverends. However, would young men like that go scrobbling the very men who'll ordain them?"

"By an aeroplane that can turn into a motorcar and then back into an aeroplane. And it can hover just like a sparrowhawk and settle down through the roof."

"Ah no, Master Kay, no aeroplane can do that."

"But I saw the aeroplane . . . I did."

At this moment the car dashed up to the door. From inside it the Chief Constable of Tatchester called, "Are you there, Drew? Come along, will you, we need every man we can get. We're to give police protection to the clergy detailed for duty in the Cathedral. Bring a truncheon, you may need it."

The Inspector unhooked a truncheon and hurried away in the car.

"He simply will not believe me," Kay said. "And in a few hours it will be too late."

He went back in deep distress to his room at Seekings.

CHAPTER TEN

'PERHAPS,' HE thought, 'if I look into the Box I may meet
with Herne the Hunter again and oh, if I do I'll ask about
Arnold of Todi, for he is the cause of all this trouble. It's his
Box and if he had it again perhaps all this hunt for it and
scrobbling folk would stop. So here goes!'

This time, as he opened the Box, it seemed to him that he
was looking between two columns on which the snow lay thick.
Here and there on the stone the snow had partly melted and had
again frozen so that little icicles dangled from the ledges. Kay
passed between these columns into a wintry wood full of snow
where even the rabbits had turned white. In front of him was
what seemed like the bole of a ruined tree, but it was Herne the
Hunter clad in some pelt, powdered with snow.

"I know what you want, Kay," he said. "You want to know

about Arnold of Todi. He went back into the Past and was caught in it somewhere and is lost, never able to get back.

"And the Past, Kay," he added, "is a big book, with many, many pages. If you go looking for Arnold in the Past, who knows if you will ever find him?"

"I have this Box. Won't this Box help me to find him?"

"No," Herne said. "Arnold left that Box behind him, because he made another way of getting back, which he liked better."

"What part of the Past d'you think he went back to?" Kay said.

"As to that," Herne answered, "there's one part that everybody goes to and that's the Trojan War."

"Could I get down to the Trojan War to ask about him?" Kay asked.

"I could get you there," Herne said, "but you must leave the Box behind you and I strongly advise you to do no such thing. You may never get back if you once get there."

"I expect I could get back," Kay said.

"Well, in a way it won't be you that goes, it will only be a shadow of you, the rest will be asleep. The you that goes will cast no shadow. People won't like that, you'll find."

"I shan't mind," Kay said.

"They may," Herne said, "and they're a pretty rough crowd in parts of the Past," Herne said, "but if you must, you must."

He beckoned to Kay and Kay felt that he became two Kays, one asleep at Seekings, the other beside Herne.

He noticed then that a sea had come almost up to where they stood. There, running into the sand at his feet, was a strange black ship, looking rather like a dolphin. The captain had a curious breastplate of some blue metal on which a wolf had been inlaid in gold.

"If you are for Troy, step on board," the captain said.

Kay stepped on board, the rowers began to row, the sail filled and the ship leaped like a dolphin. The men sang as they rowed, passing island after island, all bright in the sun, till presently they were beached on the sandy shingle between two rivers.

Kay saw on a little hill beyond them the wall of some castle from which a dense smoke was rising. As he went towards this he saw soldiers, also wearing blue breastplates with inlaid wolves. These were driving down parties of unhappy men, women and children, laden with packages of booty.

"Goodness," Kay said, "this is really Troy and I have come just too late: the city has been sacked."

Kay saw what he took to be the Tower over the Skaian Gate and looked about him at the desolation. The doors of all the houses were open; the things which had not been worth carrying away lay smashed or torn. There was nobody left in the city except a stray cat or two, mewing in misery. The pigeons which had once nested in the temples were flying about in the smoke and as Kay went up towards them a gust of wind caught the fire which burst out with a savage crackle and fierce flame. He noticed that an old, old crone was sitting at the corner of the ways. She looked as though she had been too old to be taken away.

"You are looking for Arnold of Todi?" she said. "He was here. But he has gone."

"Where did he go?" Kay asked.

"He went with the Wolves," she said.

"Has he gone long?" Kay asked.

"A matter of five hundred years ago," she said. It did not seem very hopeful to Kay, but he went back down the hill and across the ford to the beach, and there, drawing near the shore, was a boat manned by long-haired, dirty men, most of whom wore earrings. The boat had a name painted on her bows in clumsy red letters. Presently, as she drew near, Kay read this as *Seawolf*. As the boat touched the shore the man who was steering hailed him:

"Are you sick of the Mediterranean? We are."

Kay said he did not know very much about it but the man said, "You will, if you stay. Come on board."

Perhaps Kay would not have gone aboard their cutter if he had not seen that a party of spearmen, wearing breastplates stamped with the images of wolves, were slinking down the beach as though to seize him. He did not like the looks of the cutter's crew, but these Wolfmen terrified him, so he climbed aboard the cutter which at once shoved off into the sea. The Wolfmen turned back: plainly, they *had* been after him.

Kay saw that the cutter was heading for a ship in the channel. As he sat in the stern-sheets, looking at the crew, he found their eyes fixed on him. He had seen a cat looking at a little bird with that sort of look; he had heard that snakes will look at mice with that sort of look.

He looked a little anxiously towards the ship. There was a sort of green grass at her water-line and the paint had long since gone from her sides. It seemed, too, that she had been in action not long before, for splinters had been torn off her planking, leaving white wounds, sometimes jagged and irregular, sometimes round like the shot which had caused them. She was rolling slightly to the swell, her gear giving out a melancholy creak as she rolled. One of the rowers in the boat spat some tobacco juice over his shoulder and said: "She creaks, just like Old Bill after he was hanged in chains."

The boat ran alongside the ship and the stroke oar said, "Up with you, young Master." Kay clambered up the ladder to the deck. The ship had guns upon both sides of her deck and on her bulwarks little swivel guns which could be turned in any direction. On the quarter-deck just above the ship's wheel was a scroll-work which had once been gilded. Within it was a painting of the ship as she had been on her setting forth, gay with paint and hung with colours. Her name had been painted underneath in white letters: *The Bristol Merchant*. Somebody had run a streak of red paint across this name and had painted over it a new name: *The Royal Fortune*. 'I see what this is,' Kay thought. 'She is a merchant ship which has been captured by pirates.'

He had not time to think about his discovery, for with a salvo of guns the ship began to sail. Malta dropped astern in half a minute and Gibraltar a moment later. Very soon the ship was in the tropics, not far from land. There in the water were scarlet seaweeds, rainbow-coloured fishes, bits of wreck with coral stuck on them and branches with strange leaves and fruits. Kay kept away from the evil-looking men, who smoked short clay pipes and sipped rum as they sat on deck dicing.

Soon Kay saw an island rising ahead and as he watched it intently he was surprised to find one of the crew intently watching himself. Suddenly this man, who had a bloated mouth with only two front teeth in it, seized him by the collar.

"I've got you!" he said. "Here he is, boys, here's another of them."

The captain, hearing this commotion, turned and said, "What is it there?"

"It's another of them, Captain," the man said. "I've been watching him for some time and he's got no shadow."

"Bring him up in the sun," the Captain said.

They brought Kay up into the sun and stood round him with their pistols drawn, turning him about so that he caught the light.

"It's true," they said, "he's got no shadow, no more than that other one we had."

"Well, we'll soon settle him," one of the men said, drawing his cutlass and running his thumb along the edge. "One good whack with this," he said, "it'll let the shadow out that he's got tucked away inside of him."

"Hold on there, brother," another pirate said. "That's Death — it's well-known sure Death to cut a man with no shadow. Hang the sculpin up by the heels till the shadow falls out of him, *I* say."

Then another man said that it was well known that the thing

[112]

to do with a person of that sort was to shoot him with a blessed bullet. This sentiment met with general applause, but when they came to apply it to Kay they found that they had not a blessed bullet. In fact they found that the only blessed thing on board was a church candlestick, which had been in use so long for lighting pipes and warming rum that the general vote was that it was probably, by this time, not blessed, and that in any case it would be a pity to spoil the candlestick for a two-penny sculpin with no shadow.

"Wait now," the Captain said. "Once before we had one of this sort with no shadow, but we found a way of dealing with him. We marooned him on the Tiburones. There are the Tiburones! I say that we should maroon this man there too."

Kay heard one of the men say in an Irish voice, "That's a queer sort of name to give a place. What did they give it a name like that for?"

"Tiburones is its name and Tiburones is its nature," said another man. "It's the Spanish word for sharks."

Having decided Kay's fate they chained his wrists to one rail and his ankles to the other, so that he sat in great discomfort with his hands behind him and the back of his neck being scorched by the sun. After this all hands drank their rum, fired their pistols and flung seaboots at Kay's head. In a few minutes the ship glided into the quiet of the anchorage, they lowered a boat, thrust Kay into it and rowed him towards the shore. From time to time an enormous shark would heave silently alongside, just out of reach of the end of the oars. It would turn over on its back a little and show its awful mouth with the three rows of teeth.

"Now, out you get, you shadowless sculpin," the Captain said as the boat ran into the sand. They pitched Kay out head-first onto the beach. "If you look among the woods," they cried, "you may find your brother." With that the boat turned for the ship, leaving Kay alone on the desolate beach.

The sun was exceedingly hot and he was without a hat. As he

walked towards the shelter of the forest he turned to look at the ship, which was now heading for sea again. A bright flash darted from her stern port, he saw a column of water leap up from the bay, then another and then another, as the shot skimmed towards him. Just as the bang of the report reached him the shot buried itself in the beach close to where he had been standing.

"Well, here I am, marooned," Kay said to himself, keeping well under cover lest they should send another cannonball. "I wonder what I could do for food?"

There were some coconuts on some coco palms but no monkeys to hurl them to him, he saw no goats and he had no pin about him with which to make a fish-hook. Now that the ship had gone he thought that perhaps he would be able to creep down to the rocks to find shellfish, but they were so tightly stuck that he could not get them away.

He remembered reading of a sailor who used his white toes as bait, dangling them in the sea to attract a fish and then spearing them as they came to nibble. Finding a rocky pool, he drew off his shoe and stocking, slipped his foot into the water and gently waggled it about. Suddenly what seemed like the bottom of the pool rose up in a mass towards him. He snatched his foot from the water and fled, but had time to see two terrible jaws snap within an inch of his foot as he withdrew it. The worst of it was that in his hurry he knocked his shoe into the pool.

'Now I've only got one shoe,' Kay thought, 'and shipwrecked seamen have to eat their shoes . . . Oh come, animals can live on grass and leaves and things. Why shouldn't I?'

He picked some leaves, but they were so bitter that they shrivelled his mouth up. Then he picked some grass but this was very salty. He seemed to remember that some shipwrecked man of whom he had read had made elegant fish-hooks of seashells. There were many of those, but he could not find the knack of cracking them into hooks.

'Well,' he thought at last, 'perhaps this island is inhabited.

There may be people somewhere or other who will help me.'

He set off to walk through the jungle, holding his one shoe in his hand as his only supply of food. The going was extraordinarily rough, with many fallen trees and branches, but he had not gone long before a most appetising smell came to his nose. He went on with increasing hope that he would soon come to someone who would feed him. On ahead he heard the pleasant splash of falling water and at this point, somewhere beyond him in the jungle, an old man's wavering voice began to sing a song. As from the first it seemed a very queer song. Kay sat down on a fallen tree to listen to it.

"... and what is worse, I sometimes fear
It isn't Now at all that's here ...
No, but Next Year.
Next Year, or worse, some year beyond
In future time unkenned, unconned,
As far away as Trebizond
From Todi Weir.

And this I ask and fain would know:
Will Now be in a day or so?
Is this time next year Now or no?
Or did Now happen long ago,
Long, long ago?"

Reassured by something in the voice that the singer would not harm him, Kay rose from his log and pushed through the scrub until he came to a clearing where he saw the mouth of a cave, a bubbling spring falling down some rocks into a rocky pool and an old man sitting beside a fire, toasting two bananas upon skewers which he held one in each hand.

Kay limped towards the old man, who looked at him and said, "*Italiano?*" Kay shook his head.

The man said, "*Français?*"

[115]

Kay, who was on surer ground here, said, "*Non* – English."

The old man looked at him in astonishment and interest. "Come then," he said kindly, "sit, eat, drink." He took the toasted bananas from the skewers, put them on a broad leaf and offered them to Kay with a big shell full of water. Kay, who was really very, very hungry, ate the bananas with thankfulness, looking at the old man who had welcomed him. He was extraordinarily old, ragged-haired and tatter-bearded. He was dressed like a scarecrow in a most strange patchwork of palm leaves, pieces of old sail and what may once have been leather. Presently the man spoke in strange English.

"You excuse me," the man said. "Make pardon. What year in Anno Domini is this?"

"Nineteen thirty-five," Kay said.

"What you say? Nineteen – nineteen hundred?"

"Yes," Kay said, opening his hand three times and then showing four fingers. "Nineteen thirty-five."

"In the future or in the Present?"

"In the Present," Kay said.

"Oh," said the old man, "what a thing is Time. I have got lost in Time."

"Tell me please, sir," Kay said with interest, "are you Mr Arnold of Todi?"

"I was once, young Englishman," he said, "but that was when I belonged to the year of Our Lord, which I went out of by my own act. I would have none of it, I went back into the Past."

"Why did you go back into the Past?" Kay asked.

"Why?" Arnold said. "Because of the dullness of the Time in which I was born. But tell me: you, you say are English. You will please excuse and pardon. The English I have never seen. It is true that we Italians conquered the land and have a legend that the English are like rabbits in that their front teeth stick out, but that they are unlike rabbits in that they have tails. You are strange people."

"We haven't tails," Kay said.

"The fact is well known," Arnold said. "You ask me why I went back into the Past. In my young days, life in my country was tedious to a man of thought. I made a way to get back into the Past . . . a certain Box . . . you may not credit it, but a man came all the way from Spain to offer me the Elixir of Life in exchange for it. He gave me a sip of the Elixir and I let him see my Box, but I would not make the exchange."

"Do you know, I have got your Box of Delights at present," Kay said. "It belongs really to the man who came to you with the Elixir."

"It is a trivial toy," Arnold said. "I ought to have let that Spaniard take it and had his Elixir in exchange and drunken deep of it, then I could have gone on and on with Alexander. Permit me to offer you these raisins. Alexander used raisins in his campaign.

"Tell me, in the Time that you know, do they speak much of Alexander the Great?"

"He's mentioned sometimes," Kay said.

"Imagine it," Arnold said, "mentioned sometimes! Is not that typical of European things and people? Rulers and ruled alike – childish and trivial, wanting in will. What is your Christian name, young man?"

"Kay," Kay answered.

"You ought to change it to Alexander," Arnold replied. "Young men should have prosperous names, names to live up to. Kay isn't a name, it's a letter of the alphabet. It is the Greek Kappa. We Italians dispensed with it."

"Did you ever meet Alexander?" Kay asked.

"Young man," Arnold said, "I was weary of life in Todi, I made my Box and wandered into the Past of Europe. Oh, it was so dull . . . I got out of it as soon as I could. I went into the Past of Asia and suddenly, in one of those cities of Asia Minor, I first saw Alexander. You never met Alexander?"

"No indeed," Kay said, "I never did."

"He was the finest young man that ever trod this planet: beautiful, like young Apollo. The sculptors and the painters, when they wanted to carve or paint a god, all turned to him. He had only to ride down the street on that horse of his that spoke with a man's voice and every man would come out with his weapons to follow him to the world's end. Think of his god-like scheme of making the world one kingdom under one worthwhile king instead of all these little dreary kings. But of course you know of this as well as I do, you have seen Alexander . . ."

"No indeed," Kay said, "I have not."

"It is hard to believe that anyone has not seen Alexander," Arnold said, "for who knows what Beauty is that has not?" He paused for a moment, thinking of Alexander.

"I am behind in my Time, young man. I was in the Anno Domini and then I went back into the Past and the Anno Domini has moved on and I have only partly moved on, or perhaps I have moved on too far, if you understand."

"I think I do partly understand," Kay said.

"What was the race that you said you belonged to, young man?"

"The English," Kay said.

"Some very small, unimportant race," Arnold answered. "I had a list of all the nations of the world that marched with Alexander; there were no English among them. But allow me to offer you this pomegranate."

Kay ate the pomegranate, and a second one which the old man offered.

"Now, there was one special thing about Alexander that I have not told you; when I have told you this you will understand why it was that his soldiers thought that he was a god.

"We were marching across a burning waste. Whether it was the Chorasmian Waste or the Acheronian Waste, I cannot now be sure. It may perhaps have been the Gedrosian Waste. Know only that it was a burning, pitiless desert of glare and death and dead men's bones. The sand stretched, the sky arched, glare below, glare above, and the moon at night in terrible cold, with jackals howling. Some men's tongues shrivelled dry and dropped out with the parching. No water there, no drink, only pebbles and buttons to freshen our mouths with.

"Now, some of the soldiers found in a rock at dawn a little scoop of cold water. They thought, 'Now we will win promotion for ourselves by taking this to Alexander,' so they brought it to him. It was not more than is in this shell here, but in that place, under that sun, it was Life itself. Did Alexander drink it and give those men promotion? He was as thirsty as any soldier there. 'No,' he said, 'I will not touch what I cannot share with my men,' and he poured it out in the sand to his Fortune.

"Allow me now to recommend to you this egg of the island pheasant which I have baked for you. For salt, here is salt of the sea and for bread this meal of pounded almond. Eat, eat, for the young can enjoy what they eat.

"Presently, young man, I shall perfect yet another Box, much greater than any that I have made yet. I entered the Past of Europe by one Box, I entered the Past of Asia by another, but with this third Box I will go after Alexander where he rides on some planet, in some starry place in heaven. I will harness the comets for him and we will come down, young man, and we will sweep away all these paltry kings and you English with tails."

"We haven't got tails," Kay said.

"You know nothing even of your own race," Arnold said angrily, "and you dare to presume to speak of Alexander."

By this time Kay was terrified of Arnold of Todi, this extraordinary figure of fun whose matted beard was stuck with twigs and leaves and who was now standing with flaming eyes, glaring down at Kay.

'Mad as a hatter,' Kay thought. 'Now he will probably tear me piecemeal.'

At this instant he heard himself called: "Kay! Kay!" There behind him in a little bay of the sea, so bright and beautiful, were two figures whom he saw to be Herne the Hunter and the Woman of the Oak Tree. On their left hands were those curious rings with the longways crosses upon them.

"Come, Kay," they said. "We can take you home. You must not be lost in the Past in this way."

"Could you take Arnold of Todi too?" he said. "He has been most awfully kind to me."

"Yes," they said, "let him come."

Kay did not quite see how they were to come, but when they reached the beach the two called and out of the sea there came tumbling the most beautiful dolphins, drawing a chariot made of one big sea-shell of the colour of mother-of-pearl.

By the side of these were three bigger dolphins, one with no saddle for Herne the Hunter, two with high-backed saddles of white and scarlet coral and stirrups and reins of amber beads, for Kay and Arnold.

"You will mount these, Kay," the lady said, as she stepped into her chariot and gathered the long reins of seaweed, "then follow me."

Kay, Herne and Arnold mounted and at once the dolphins leaped from the water, plunged in and again leaped out, on the long rush towards home, while the woman called to the team and sang to them:

"Come, flying-fish, come, whales,
Come, mermaids with bright scales,
Come, gulls that ride on gales,
And albatrosses
That no gale tosses."

As they sped, the mermaids shot to the surface beside them, many white, grey and gleaming birds swooped out of heaven to them, the whales surged out from below, snorting out glittering fountains. With little whickering flickers the flying-fish leaped beside them like tiny silver arrows. It was exquisite to feel the dolphins quivering to the leap, and to surge upwards into the bright light with flying-fish sparkling on each side; then to surge down into the water, scattering the spray like bright fire. In the thrill and delight of this leaping journey Kay fell asleep. He was presently aware of Arnold getting off his dolphin at Tibbs Wharf near the Lock and Key. He half opened his eyes, thought he heard the church bells chime and then woke up drowsily at Seekings, under the valance of the dressing-table, where the Box lay on the floor. He went down to lunch.

"Well, Kay," Jemima said after a while, "you have seemed to be half-asleep ever since lunch began. Aren't you going to say something?"

"Say something?" Kay said. "Where is Arnold?"

"Arnold?" they said. "Who's Arnold?"

"It's very odd," Kay said, and went to the window to pull himself together. There, at the top of the garden, was a strange figure of fun, dressed seemingly in old leather, bits of sail and palm-leaf, staring with admiration at the church tower.

Kay hurried out to speak to him, but he was no longer there.

CHAPTER ELEVEN

W HEN HE returned to the house Maria had a special edition of the Tatchester paper.

"Kay," she said, "you're losing all the fun. They've tried to scrobble another clergyman who was walking in to Tatchester from Tineton."

"Did they get him?" Kay asked.

"No, they didn't get him," Maria said. "Here is the account. I'll read it:

CHURCH BANDITS FOILED

It now seems undoubted that the recent outrages at Tatchester are the work of an organised gang. We are happy to state that on this occasion the scoundrels were defeated. The Reverend Josiah Stalwart, Rector of

Tineton, had undertaken in answer to the Bishop's plea to be prepared in case of need to help with the services in the Cathedral tonight. While proceeding to Tatchester along the Roman road he was passed by a dark motorcar in which were two men who got out and asked if he would like a lift. Not quite liking their looks and being naturally on his guard in view of recent events, he declined the lift and at once the taller man attempted to fling over his head what seemed like a felt bag, while the accomplice tried to deal him a short-arm punch in the ribs. The Reverend Stalwart avoided the felt bag and smote his shorter assailant on the head with the holly cudgel which had been lately presented to him by his admiring colleagues of the Tineton Hockey Team. The ruffians, realising too late the kind of man with whom they had to deal, darted into the car, the engine of which had been kept running, and were at once out of sight, going at great speed.

Needless to say, the precautions of the Police have been trebled on every road leading to Tatchester. In future no clergyman will proceed to Tatchester to take Christmas duty save under Police protection.

We understand that the Tineton Hockey Club has sent a long telegram of congratulation to their victorious captain.

"You see," Maria said, "they've been diddled this time. The Reverend Josiah must be a bit of a boy to take on two."

Kay went back to his room, thinking, 'They've had a good deal of success, but this setback, coming at this time, will make Abner furious and he may proceed to extremes. I must find out what he intends to do.'

It was now very nearly half-past two. Kay went back to his room, locked himself in and crawled underneath the valance of the dressing-table. He turned the knob of the Box so that he might go, both swift and little, to Abner's room at Chester Hills.

He was set down in the upper corridor of the Theological College, near a door that stood ajar under the little label 'Chief'. Kay listened near this door but nobody seemed to be within. He peeped in: no one was there. He slipped inside and then, as he wished to examine the room, he resumed his proper shape and closed the door. Then, suddenly, he heard voices just outside.

Abner was saying, "But I left this door ajar!"

A key pressed into the lock, giving Kay just time to press the knob of his Box so that he might go small when the door opened and Abner and Joe came in. Kay squeezed into a recess by the fireplace.

"Funny thing about that door," Abner said, "I left it ajar purposely. Someone's been in here and left the window open. Do you know who's been in?"

"No, Chief," Joe said, "of course I don't."

"No 'of course' about it," Abner snapped. "Now then, listen to me. Who sent those two fools to tackle Josiah Stalwart?"

"I did," Joe growled.

"Didn't I give strict orders that no scrobbling party was to consist of less than four."

"That was before we were short-handed."

"Did I or did I not give those orders?"

"Now Chief," Joe said, "chuck it. I'd have sent four after Stalwart if I'd have had four to send. You never told us Stalwart was a champ. You told me I was to get him scrobbled and I did what we could. If you had seen Eleven and Twelve before Seventeen dressed their wounds you might feel a little sorry for them."

"What did Stalwart do to them, two against one?"

"He cracked Twelve's crown across a fair treat. He gave Eleven an eye like a stained-glass window. They're marked for a month, the pair of them."

"And a jolly good job," Abner said. "I wish Stalwart had given them a cauliflower ear. I wish he'd knocked their silly noses west and banged their ribs blue and yours, too."

"Chief," Joe said, "we'll set that aside if you don't mind. While you've been in Tatchester I've been thinking of things and I've made up my mind."

"So you made up your mind, did you?" Abner asked.

"Yes, Chief, I did."

"I didn't know you had a mind, but I'm glad to hear it. And so you've made it up?"

"Yes, Chief, I have."

"What did you decide?" Abner asked.

"Tomorrow's Christmas Day."

"So I hear. What about it?"

"Christmas Day's rather a special day. We don't like keeping all those poor captives away from their homes on Christmas Day."

"*We* don't like. Who are *we*?"

"All the lot of us. We want you to return all the captives tonight, by air, with a ten-pound note apiece, the ones we got at the bank robbery. Then the whole thing would pass off as a rag . . . and it would tell in our favour if we ever came to be tried. And there's another thing we've got to speak about," Joe continued stubbornly.

"*Got* to speak about," Abner said. "Then speak it . . . proceed."

"I've been telling them about your magic and that," Joe said. "What we don't see is why you don't use magic to find this Box that you set such store by."

"You don't believe in magic, I think, but perhaps this may convince you," Abner said. "Watch now . . ."

He lifted his hand in a strange way and uttered some foreign words in a loud, clear voice. Instantly the figure of a boy with a bony, unintelligent and unpleasant face, appeared through Abner's desk.

[125]

"What d'ye want me for now?" he growled.

"No pertness," Abner said. "Tell the gentleman what Cole Hawlings did with his Box."

"He gave it to somebody to keep for him," the Boy said. "I told you that before."

"Learn civility," Abner said. "To whom did he give it?"

"I don't know. He put spells round it. I couldn't see the person. Let me go."

"If you're not careful and civil I'll peg you into a waterfall," Abner said. "Am I nearer to getting the Box than I was?"

"Yes. You're very near to it," the Boy said.

"Shall I get it?"

"You'll have it under your hand today. Now I want to go – I've told you everything."

"Don't try to dictate to me," Abner said. "The gentleman would like to ask you something. Ask him anything you want to know, Joe."

Joe did not much relish speaking to the Boy, but at last he asked:

"What is in this Box?"

"The way in to the Past. I will not be questioned by you."

"Yes, you will," Abner said. "Anything else, Joe?"

"Yes," Joe said. "What will win the National?"

"Kubbadar, by seven lengths. Now I'm going."

"Wait, my young insolent friend," Abner said. "You will have a little lesson before you go."

As the Boy approached Abner tapped him on the top of the head with a timetable. The head at once telescoped into the chest and the legs telescoped into his body.

"Off now," Abner said. "You'll stay plugged under the waterfall for seven weeks for insolence. Perhaps that may teach you!"

The Boy vanished into the desk, howling loudly from the middle of his chest.

Abner touched something in the corner over his head, then

went to the hearthrug and stamped upon it with some force. There came a clicking, clacking noise and Kay saw the fireplace slide open like a door, revealing a lift lit with an electric light.

"Come on, then," Abner said.

The two men stepped into the lift and Kay darted after them as the fireplace closed to. Abner pressed a red button in the lift wall and the lift slowly began to move down. When it stopped the Chief opened the door and Kay followed as he and Joe stepped out.

He was in a wide, high cavern or gallery stretching to right and left in the rock. Kay heard water dropping, drop by drop like the tick of a very slow clock and saw what seemed like a range of ship's cabins stretching along the side of the gallery. Abner went to the door of the first of these, pulled aside a shutter, turned on a light to light the cell within and spoke through the opening:

"And how is the dear Bishop?" he said. "Christmas sermon getting on well? Well, well, well! And will you tell me where the package is?"

"I tell you, ruffian," the Bishop answered, "that I know nothing of any package. These pleasantries had better cease."

"Tell me where the package is," Abner said, "and they shall cease and starvation shall cease and you shall have a savoury omelet and coffee and rolls and honey. What, you won't? Water from the well, then, and darkness to meditate upon it."

He switched out the light, fastened the shutter and moved to another door.

"Dean," he said, "still cheerful? Splendid! Can you tell me of the package yet? What, you don't know anything about it? That won't do for me, my Dean, think again. Keep cheerful."

He went from cell to cell asking the inmates where the Box was. Some said, "We don't know what you mean," others said, "You are mad. The Police will soon run you down, to be sure."

"Don't you be too sure," Abner said. "And here, I think, are the Canons Minor. How that brings back my Latin – major, minor, minimus! And are my Minor Canons going to tell me of the package?"

By this time Abner had reached the end of the cells. Raising his voice so that he could be heard all along the gallery, "So you are all stubborn," he said. "You'll find that I'm stubborn and the rock is stubborn and not all the Police in Europe could find you where you are now. One of you knows where this package is. Tell me and you shall be at home within the day. If not, I can last and the rock will last, but I don't think you will."

He turned to Joe, who was at his side.

"By the way, Joe," he said, still in his loud voice, "this cell at the end here – we put the Earl into it, you remember, because he wouldn't pay the ransom. Seven years ago, I think it was – you remember?"

"I remember well," Joe said. "A dark, handsome man, the Earl – very well-dressed."

"That's the man," Abner said, unlocking the cell door. "Just step in, will you, and see if his bones are still there?"

Kay saw Joe step into the lighted cell and pretend to rummage in the corners.

"Just the skull and a rib or two," Joe said. "Oh, and his marriage ring."

"Quite so," said Abner, locking him into the cell and switching out the light. "And now, my dear Joe with the made-up mind, meditate with these holy men on the errors of your ways. Another time you may not be so brave as to tell me that I am making a mistake."

Joe beat upon the door, shouting threats and curses as Abner moved away, whistling a few bars of Schubert's Unfinished Symphony. Kay, who was horror-struck, moved away after him, running where Abner's footsteps led. Suddenly, from a cell not yet visited, Peter's voice piped up.

"If you please," Peter said, "I think I know where the package that you want is."

"Ha," Abner said, "so! And where is the package?"

"I can't explain it," Peter said, "but I could take you there, if you want."

"Oh, could you?" Abner said. "And give us the slip on the way, no doubt. We are not quite so green. Where is it?"

"If you please, I thought I saw a package just before they scrobbled the Punch and Judy man up on Bottler's Down."

"Ha," Abner said, "you thought wrong then; think again . . . and think of mushrooms for breakfast. Have you thought of them?"

"Yes, sir," Peter said.

"Well, that's all the breakfast you'll get," Abner said.

He moved away up the gallery so rapidly that Kay could hardly keep pace. As he came near Joe's cell, Joe cried:

"I say, old man, a joke's a joke but don't leave an old pal here in the dark – not old Joe, Abner."

"Yes, old Joe," Abner replied. He had gone past Joe's cell when something seemed to strike him. "By the way, Joe," he said, "you don't believe in magic, do you?"

Out of the air came little faces, grinning and wicked, with pointed ears and pointed teeth. They flitted swiftly through the bars of Joe's cell and buzzed round Joe's head. Joe beat at them as though they were wasps, but they were too quick to be hit. Abner watched the effect of these imps upon Joe's terror-stricken face.

"No, he doesn't believe in magic, Joe doesn't," he said. "However, take your time. You will, presently." He switched out the light and marched on, turning swiftly up a gallery which Kay had not noticed. Presently he opened the door into a lighted room and Kay slipped in behind him before the door closed.

It was a bare room, carpeted with a thick red carpet and with certain strange magical symbols painted on the walls in red. In the middle of the room on a pedestal was a bronze head, its eyelids closed, drooping as though asleep. As Abner lifted his right hand the eyelids opened, the head raised itself, the lips moved and a voice said, "Command me, Master."

"Tell me of our plans," Abner said.

The voice spoke from the head: "Your agents have now captured every clergyman attached to the Cathedral, as well as most of the Cathedral servants and staff."

"Is anything going wrong?"

"Yes," the bronze head replied. "You should have begun (as I told you) much later in the day. You have given them time to act against you."

"Don't criticise me, Slave," Abner said. The head at once cowered down upon the pedestal and began to whimper.

"Stop that," Abner said. "Tell me now, what are they trying to do against me?"

"All sorts of things," the head said. "Mainly telephoning and telegraphing, trying to get substitutes."

"With what success?" Abner said.

"Not much yet," the head said. "It is Christmas. All the clergy are busy in their own parishes, but substitutes will be found. There is a body of Friends of the Cathedral – I told you of them: the Tatchester Trusties, they are the ones. They will rake up clergy from all sorts of places, you will see."

"Will I?" Abner said. "Will they? We'll try that."

He raised his hand in a peculiar manner. Instantly a red-winged figure rose up out of the floor and bowed before him.

"Cut all the Tatchester telephone and telegraph wires," he said. "Wait. Bring in those Tatchester Trusties."

"I go, sir," the winged figure said, disappearing through the ceiling.

"That won't see you very far," the brazen head said. "Some of the substitute clergy have already started."

Abner raised his right hand again and another red figure rose from the floor.

"Command me, Master," it said.

"Dislocate all railway traffic for twenty miles round Tatchester. Jam the points."

"I go, sir," the figure answered, disappearing through the ceiling.

"That won't be much use," the bronze head said. "They will come by road."

Abner raised his hand again. A third red figure rose from the floor and asked for orders.

"Make every road impassable for twenty miles round Tatchester," he said. "But stay, that won't be enough. We must make the air impassable too. One moment."

He lifted his left hand in a strange way and an old, old crone was thrust through the floor by little red hands towards him. She looked so old that she might have been a thousand years or more: nose and chin almost met, her face was the colour of old wood. She seemed terrified of Abner.

"What d'you want with me, Master?" she said.

"I want a storm out of the north and the east," Abner said, "with snow."

"I can't give it, I can't give it," the old woman said. "You ask too much. I can only sell a storm for a great sum – a bag of amethyst."

"I will give you a quarter bag," Abner said. "Now let me have the storm."

He produced from his pocket a little canvas bag which did contain amethysts: Kay saw the stones as he emptied them out, a very meagre quarter, which was handed to the old woman. She in turn produced from her pocket a little leather bag tied with three strings at the mouth.

"Don't open more than two of those strings," the old woman said warningly, "or you may be sorry."

"Don't tell me how I am to proceed," Abner said. "Away with her!" At once the little red hands plucked the old woman away.

"Servant, here!" Abner cried to the red figure. "Away with this to Tatchester. Open two strings from the mouth of this bag and fill the roads and the air with snow so that neither cars nor aeroplanes shall come near Tatchester. Let any clergyman that tries to get there be buried six feet in snow and not be found until the spring."

"He cannot do that," the brazen head said. "He cannot take life."

"Do not interrupt me, you," Abner said. "As for you, Servant, take that bag, open the third string and flood the countryside with the deepest snow since Wolves ran. Make the drifts eight feet deep round each Cathedral door. Away with you!"

"I go, sir," the figure said and vanished through the ceiling.

Abner turned to the brazen head.

"You have interrupted me, you have criticised me," he said. "All this establishment seems given over to mutiny. I will have you learn respect. You shall be upside-down for a while."

"I implore you, Master, not," the head said, whimpering.

"I say yes," Abner said, and plucking the head from its pedestal he jammed it violently down upon it upside-down, where it whimpered and wailed.

"Shut up," Abner said. "Listen to me and tell me truth: am I to have that Box today?"

"You will have it under your hand," the head said.

"Ha," Abner said. "Who will bring me the Box?"

Kay was by this time trembling lest the head should know where the Box was at the moment. It was at that instant that the poor upside-down eyes caught sight of the tiny figure of Kay near the door. The eyes showed astonishment, then excitement. 'He'll betray me now,' Kay thought, 'so as to be turned right-side up again.' Then he saw that the head was rebelling against Abner for being turned upside-down, for one of the eyes winked at Kay to reassure him.

"What are you rolling your eyes for?" Abner asked.

"You'd roll *your* eyes if you were upside-down," the head said.

"Is the Box near?"

"It is very near."

"Right," Abner said. "Now, mend your manners there."

He strode swiftly out of the room, Kay following at once to avoid being shut in. Following on as fast as he could, he heard something which made his heart leap:

"So, Miss Caroline Louisa," Abner was saying in some dark den in the rock, "you would not tell me about the Box, though you must know all about it. Now you may like to know that it is on its way to me; nothing can stop its coming to me."

Caroline Louisa did not answer, but Kay heard her cough and knew that she was there. Abner came striding back past Kay, there came a sudden noise of a door rolling in a groove and the cave became bright with light.

Kay saw that a door in the rock had slid back and beyond it a curious motorcar, thickly sprinkled with snow, was being opened by masked men who dragged from it two figures whose arms and legs were lashed and whose heads were in felt bags.

"Ha," Abner said, "the Tatchester Trusties, I presume. Working, no doubt, double time like good friends of the Cathedral to find clergy for the services. Excellent work, but it must now be interrupted for the time. First action, then contemplation. Remove them to the cells."

In deep thought, Abner moved along the rocky gallery. Kay heard a continual murmur of water falling, but soon judged that this noise was not from falling water but from violent sobbing and lamenting. When they came near to the noise Abner turned on a light.

"Ha," said Abner, "my vocal and orchestral friends from Tatchester! The choir, I think? And is our cocoa as you like it? And do you admire our brand of bun? Now listen to me, boys. There is something very disgusting to me in the undisguised grief of boys who do not carry handkerchiefs and use the backs of their hands. Stop snivelling, you little beasts! Now, which of you has the Box of Delights and where is it?"

[133]

Some of the elder members of the choir asked him what on earth he meant.

"Very well then," Abner said, "you have had your chance – your bloods will be on your own heads – you are doomed. Midnight will soon strike on the Cathedral clock and there will be no service in the Cathedral – no! For the Cathedral staff will be rolling:

> Where Alph, the sacred river, swishes,
> With Organist and boys and Bishes,
> Down to a sunless sea."

He walked away, followed by threats from the Organist, cries from the baritones and basses and piteous wails from the choirboys.

The voices and crying died as Abner sped swiftly into the recesses of the cavern, walking by the aid of a torch which he flashed on from time to time. Kay, on his little tiny feet, had to hurry as best he could after the flashes. Sometimes he fell into some pit in the floor and bumped himself, sometimes he ran into a projecting stone and bruised himself. He felt to the full the misery of being tiny.

Presently Abner turned on a light by which Kay saw that they were in a broad gallery, in the side of which, backed against a rock, was a cage of strong iron bars raised a little from the floor. In the midst of the cage, heavily chained, was old Cole Hawlings.

Abner walked up to within a few feet of the bars.

"Master Cole," he said, "or Master Lully: Great Master, the time has come for us to speak together. You are so beset by my power that you can never escape from here without my leave. I come to tell you that the Box is now on its way to me. Nothing can stop its coming.

"Once, long ago, you walked from Spain to Italy to buy the Box with your Elixir of Life. I will sell you the Box for the Elixir. Will you deal?"

"No," Cole said, "because you are a greedy scoundrel, unfit to have long life."

"I will repeat the offer once more," Abner said, "but only once. After that, you will see."

As he turned away up the gallery Kay swung himself into the fold of Abner's turned-up trouser, where he was tossed and banged by the rapid going until Abner stopped, unlocked a strongroom, entered and shut the door to behind him. It was a stronger room than any that Kay had thought possible. No sound of any sort came within it, as if the walls were more than a foot thick, of solid iron. It was brightly lit, about nine feet high and twelve feet across. On one side there was a small sofa with cushions, on another a table on which stood an open iron deed-box. Abner went to the table and burrowed in the open box.

"Yes," he said, "we have done not badly at all with our little ventures. When the Box of Delights comes I can sail with these to my quiet island. Ramon Lully will see wisdom, he will grant me the Elixir too before I go. But I must have a look at these once more."

He felt at the door to be sure that it was closed.

"Strange," he muttered, "that little boy, Kay Harker, why should he come into my mind? He'd better not come into my presence!" At this he produced from his hip pocket a pistol which he put upon the table beside him. Kay slipped from the trouser-end to the floor, where he could watch.

Abner opened one of the bags in the deed-box.

"Ah, the Duke's rubies!" he said. "The setting is rather coarse, but they are a rare crimson. And these – these emeralds and these pearls. We have done well in pearls and they are very light – very light to carry. And these are my sapphires – blue and yellow: my favourite stone." Kay saw him turn out a little bag of sapphires on to the table. "Ah, I could never part with these," he muttered. "There is something about this blue and this yellow. Why anybody should prefer other stones I cannot think. But now for the real box – the rich box."

Kay watched him open a silver jewel-box which contained what looked like rolls of brown paper, some of which he unrolled. Kay could see the glitter of pendants, necklaces, coronets and stars of glittering diamonds. Abner chuckled as he played with them.

"All the clever jewel thieves in this world," he muttered, "have worked for little Abner getting these. There must be a matter of three hundred thousand in this little box alone. I shall retire. It's enough, even for me."

There was a pause. "Strange," he said, "strange! That little mildew of a boy is in my thoughts the whole time. I think I will take a nap, that will do me good."

Kay saw him slip off his shoes, lie down upon the sofa, shake the pillows a little and fall instantly asleep. There Kay was, shut up in the strong-room for what seemed like hours while Abner slept.

'What shall I do?' Kay thought. 'I know, I'll go to Caroline Louisa and ask her advice.'

He had only to twirl the knob and speak his wish to be whirled to the corridor where she was prisoned, but here he found himself beset by magic. He called, but she did not hear; he groped, but could not find the prison; heavy felt blankets came in his way, tripped him up and baffled him. Besides these, horrid little aeroplanes with snouts like wolves came snapping at him. He was soon glad to wish himself back in Abner's strong-room, where he found Abner just waking from his nap.

"I *have* had a sleep," he said. "Come on now."

He took the deed-box from the table and laid it on the floor close to Kay. Then he knelt down and unpacked its contents. Some of the bags of jewels almost fell upon Kay, who trembled in every limb lest he should be seen.

'What shall I do?' Kay thought. 'I must stay here to learn more of this place if I am to rescue the others.'

He lay still, hoping that Abner would not see, but Abner was intent upon the jewels.

He took some packages from a shelf, removed some of the packages already packed and began to re-stow the box. "No," he said when he had finished, "even now it won't do. I must get some amethysts in."

He pitched some of the packages onto the floor, poured loose amethysts into the box, shook it to make them settle down and then snatched packages from the floor and crammed them in on top. In his hurry he picked up Kay with one of the packages, pitched him into the box, jammed him down tight, so that Kay's bones were nearly smashed, and then squeezed him fast with a couple of packages. Then he shut the lid, sat on it to make it close, locked it, passed a chain round the outside of it, apparently secured the chain with a padlock, then lifted it with a jerk and banged it down on the table with a jolt, so that Kay was shaken, squeezed, banged, bruised and battered as though the coals had been delivered on top of him. By kicking and struggling he managed to reach the top of the heap, so that he could breathe what little air there was.

"This is enough for me," he muttered. "I will go home." Struggling hard, he contrived to move his arms and felt in his pocket for the Box, but alas, it was no longer there: it must have been jolted out as he struggled among the jewel bags. The precious Box was gone. There he was, no bigger than a mouse, perhaps forty miles from home, in a strong-room in a prison in the rock, padlocked and chained within a locked iron box, which was perhaps soon to be carried to some distant island. He heard a cork drawn, then he heard Abner apparently cracking walnuts. There came the glug-glug of something poured from a bottle and he heard Abner's teeth crunching nuts and his lips smacking over his drink.

"A very pretty little port," Abner was saying. "A little lacking in body, but a pleasant afternoon drink."

Kay heard the glug-glug repeated more than once, then

Abner picked up the deed-box from the table and shook it.

"Ah," he said, "not many people shake half a million pounds of jewels at one go. Soon I shall be aboard the submarine, speeding through the billows. Oh, happy Abner!

"And to think of all the benefits I have conferred, the stimulus that I have given to the jewel trade. Half the noble families of Europe have had to buy new jewels because of me. Then too, the benefit that I conferred upon the Church. Now, at one swoop, the curate becomes a rector, the rector a canon, the canon an archdeacon, the archdeacon a dean, and the dean a bishop. Think, too, what I do to the tourist industry! Thousands will come to Tatchester to see the scene of the recent outrages – and this romantic pile here will be all water underneath and charred ashes above. I will open the sluices now. I have emptied six gallons of petrol in the older parts of the house downstairs, where the wood is driest. A wax Vesta on my return from Tatchester will suffice for that. With what splendour shall I pass from here! A gurgling flood deep down in the cave and a roaring bonfire above."

Kay heard Abner open the strong-room door, which he slammed-to behind him. He set out, walking fast, swinging the deed-box to and fro and singing light-heartedly. Each swing drove hard knobs in the bags onto some part of poor Kay, who rolled this way and that, almost suffocated, and was forced to lie face downwards with arms outspread to keep from being shaken under the bags.

CHAPTER TWELVE

PRESENTLY KAY realised that Abner had reached a lift. He heard the grille thrust back, then closed, and felt the lift start. When it stopped at the top of the shaft they came out into what Kay judged to be Abner's bedroom.

"Hurray, hurray," Abner carolled. "No more of the worry of thinking for all these fools." He put the Box upon his table.

"How it is snowing," he muttered. "I wonder what fool left my window open. There is a foot of snow on my pillow, but there is no doubt about this being a storm. No clergy will get to Tatchester through this."

Kay heard him slam the window to.

"One moment," Abner muttered to himself, "it might be just as well if I heard what my merry mariners are up to. They aren't exactly the kind of lads to trust further than there's need.

I'll tune in the wireless to their mess deck."

Kay heard Abner turn a switch and there came a confused growling murmur of knives and forks and conversation, somebody pounded a bottle on a table and a voice said, "And now, gents, our gallant captain, known to his enemies as Death-Chops but to us as Rum-Chops, is kindly going to oblige with a song of his own make about one we all wot of. Pray silence for our great commander's melodious joy."

There were loud cheers, Kay heard a chair pushed back, Rum-Chops cleared his throat and at once burst into his melodious joy:

"Our Abner is a captain bold,
    the nimblest ever seen-o.
He thinks to fly with all his gold
    Aboard our submarine-o,
To leave his gang to wreck or hang,
    or languish in a gaol-o."

Loud cheers followed this ditty.

"That is very clever of Rum-Chops," Abner muttered. "I had not given him credit for so much wit. So he has guessed that I'm leaving for good."

As the coarse laughter, cheers, banging of pots, table-pounding, guffaws and stamping of feet died away, Rum-Chops called, "Now, will you all load your pistols and charge your glasses: we'll give the last chorus fiery honours. Are you all ready now . . . ?"

There came the glug-glug of rum pouring from bottles and the click of many pistol-hatches being snapped and re-snapped. "All ready, Governor," several voices said.

"I wonder what is to follow," Abner muttered. He was not long left in doubt. Rum-Chops pounded the table with a bottle and began:

"This may be nice for Abner Brown,
    but not so nice for us-o,
And so we plan to let him drown
    without unpleasant fuss-o.
When the submarine is seething green
    And the water's far from shoal-o,
We'll weight his heels for all his squeals
    and drop him through a hole-o."

All through the stanza there had been sounds of ill-suppressed joy, but when Rum-Chops reached the last line, bang went all the pistols, crash went all the glasses, there were yells and cheers and the last two lines were repeated and repeated.

At last, as the noise abated, the voice of Rat, much excited and rather confused, was heard saying, "I know another line what we could sing."

"What line is that?" someone asked.

Rat gurgled with laughter. "You'll die laughing at it," he said, "this is what it is but I don't know that I can for laughing:

Ho, something . . . diddle and diddle and
    something . . . and something diddle
           and Olo.

That's what."

There was a long, awful silence, then Kay heard one of the pirates say:

"Where's that nephew of his? Here, Alf Rat, help your uncle up to bed."

Abner turned off the wireless set with a click.

"So," he said, "mutiny, even here. I rather feared it. No matter, they shall pay the penalty and I will go to my island by aeroplane.

"And now," he went on, "now for the great moment. Now for my Pouncer. Much as I have suffered from these fools, I have suffered more from my sweet Pouncer, but to make sure of my sweet Pouncer will be but the work of half an hour."

So saying, he left the room, singing a little ditty. The clock ticked slowly. It struck for a half-hour, then for ten o'clock, then for half-past ten, but Abner did not return. When Kay heard the door open he thought it would be Abner, but two people came in.

"You see, my Pouncer, what," a familiar voice said, "I told you he was going to put a double-cross on us. There is the boodle, all packed up."

"False-hearted, treacherous Abner," the Pouncer said.

"Ha-ha, what," the foxy-faced man replied. "My master-key will soon resolve the matter." Kay heard him unlock the padlock on the chain and then the deed-box. "Ha-ha, you see, what," the foxy-faced man said, thrusting back the lid. "Cat's-eyes, diamonds, pearls, emeralds, rubies – everything. Even the special blue and yellow sapphires."

"Never shall he look upon them again," the Pouncer said. "Quick, into our suitcase."

"They are going to fly together," Kay thought.

In their hurry and excitement they did not notice Kay, but thrust bag after bag of jewels into the suitcase.

"Wait, you have left something," the Pouncer said.

"Ah, it is only a bit of rag," the foxy-faced man answered. It was not a bit of rag: it was poor, trembling Kay at the bottom of the box. The foxy-faced man picked him up between thumb and forefinger and pitched him into the grate, where luckily he fell into the ashes, not into the fire. "It was only a bit of old chamois," the foxy-faced man said. "A bit of jeweller's rag. Now we had better be off."

"Wait," the Pouncer said. "Fill the box up with coal."

"My Sylvia, what an inspiration," the foxy-faced man said. "Never was your equal born."

Nimbly he placed some big lumps of coal from the scuttle in the deed-box, carefully muffling their jolting with a towel and a tablecloth.

"My dear Charles, you think of everything," the Pouncer said.

"Who would not, inspired by Sylvia," he answered, taking up the keys. "Now, swift . . . there it is, locked . . . there is the chain . . . and there, finally, the padlock. Beautiful, and no traces left."

"And now, away, my Charles," the Pouncer said.

"Wait yet, my Sylvia," the foxy-faced man answered. "He has put old Joe in one of the dungeons. We must set old Joe free first. Did you ever see his Zoo?"

"I never did," the Pouncer said.

"You shall now," the foxy-faced man said. "We'll have time before the Police are here."

Kay saw them work the mechanism of the lift and disappear within it. As soon as they were gone he crawled out of the grate, which was unpleasantly hot. He was crouching in a corner of the room when he heard the lift draw near. Sylvia, Charles and Joe came out, Sylvia wearing nine diamond necklaces.

"There's the box that he packed the boodle in," Charles said, pointing to the deed-box.

"I'll boodle him, the beauty," Joe said. "What can I do against him, I wonder?"

"Oh, come along, Joe," Charles said.

"I'll put my boot through his window first," Joe said.

He kicked through each pane: snow came driving in in a cloud.

Sylvia Pouncer peered into the fireplace. "Didn't you throw away a bit of chamois, Charles?" she asked. "I'd like it now, if you could find it, to give my diamonds a rub with."

Charles peered into the grate beside her. "It was just a bit of dirty chamois," he said, "like a little rag, what? I'm afraid it went into the fire and got burned. It doesn't seem to be there now. Perhaps we'd better come along now. Come along, Joe."

"I shall never find the Box again now," Kay said to himself. "If it's in the deed-box Abner will find it, as the Boy said he would, and if it isn't in the deed-box it is probably in one of those bags which they are carrying. They've been sharing the spoils, evidently. There is just a chance that it has been spilled out onto the floor here . . . oh, I do hope it has."

He looked, with a beating heart, but could not see it. While he was looking the door of the room opened and Abner came in.

"Confound this window," he said. "The snow's drifted in all over the place again and broken the window, too. Where on earth has the Pouncer got to? Well, I must get going and leave that deed undone."

He picked up the deed-box. As he did so Kay swung himself once more into the turned-up trouser-end. Abner took the lift down to the gallery and walked swiftly to Cole's cage, where he put down the box, sat upon it and spoke.

"Now, Ramon, or Cole, my merry old soul," he said. "I have only one thing to say to you: I want your Elixir. How about it?"

"No," Cole said, "nothing that you can offer shall buy the Elixir from me. You are unfit to possess it."

"You realise the alternative," Abner said. "If I am not to have the Elixir, be sure that you will not profit from it. You see this iron wheel in the rock face? It works sluices by which I can flood these cellars at will. Your box for your Elixir . . . it is a fair exchange."

"You have nothing with which to bargain," Cole answered. "You say that you have my Box, or will have it. You are wrong, you will not have it."

"Very good then," Abner said. "The water shall come in." He took the wheel and was about to swing it round when a thought seemed to strike him.

"Wait one moment," Abner said. "I confess I do set a little store by your Elixir of Life. You are not ignorant of Magic. If you see my Helper, you will hear from him that your Box of Delights will be mine before midnight. That may convince you." He lifted his hand in the familiar way and there came a noise of dripping as in the corridor appeared that Boy whom

Abner had smitten with the timetable. The creature's head was still deep within his chest, his legs were still telescoped into his body, but his sulkiness and pertness were gone. He was dripping wet.

"So," Abner said, "the waterfall has taken some of the insolence from you, it would seem. Now, tell this gentleman the truth. The Box that I search for, shall I not have it by midnight?"

"No," the Boy whimpered.

"You told me that I should have it," Abner said.

"I didn't," the Boy said. "I said you'd have it under your hand and you've had it under your hand. You've had it under your hand for something like an hour this afternoon and you didn't know. Now it isn't under your hand and it won't be under your hand again and you don't know where it is and you'll never know where it is."

"Tell me instantly where it is," Abner said.

"I won't tell you another thing more," the Boy said. "You can peg me under the waterfall, or melt me in the fire, or bury me, or blow me through the winds, yet I'll never tell you another thing, except that you had the Box and didn't know it and now you won't have it again, ever. So that's what I call Squish to you."

Abner smote the Boy on his neck and Kay saw him telescope up under the blow: this time his legs went right through his body and out of the shoulders.

"Get you back to your waterfall," Abner said, "and you will stay there for seven years."

At this moment Kay saw Cole Hawlings in the cage lifting his right hand in spite of his irons. As he did so the Boy slowly began to untelescope: the legs went down, the body rose up from the legs, the neck and head rose up from his chest, till there he was, a boy again, looking rather less bony and unpleasant than he had looked in Abner's study.

"Well, I shan't," the Boy said to Abner, "I shan't be pegged under the waterfall, for I've been set free, see, from you and yours. A jolly good Squish to you. Squish, Abner!" At this he suddenly became fainter and disappeared upwards.

"You see," Cole Hawlings said, "you have deceived yourself. The Box will not be yours, nor shall my secret be yours, whatever happens to myself."

"Very well," Abner said, "I am not to have your Elixir, it seems, and I am not to have your Box, but I shall have something and that's revenge on you, for I am going to drown you, Cole Hawlings, like a rat in a trap."

He seized the wheel and spun it round. Kay heard a distant clattering noise, a thud, and then a great, fierce but still distant roaring rush of water.

"You hear," Abner said, "the sluice is working beautifully. There's a great head of water in the lake: thirty feet of dammed-back flood-water is coming after you. It won't take very long to reach you. And now I shall set off with my little earnings to a place of rest and beauty."

"You will not set off," Cole answered. "All the exits to this place are now guarded by Police."

"No Police can guard the exit by which I shall go," Abner answered. "Goodbye, sleep well, Cole."

He kissed his hand to his victim and as he turned to walk away Kay slipped from the folded trouser-end; he had had enough of Abner.

Abner whistled to his guard of little Wolves that were yapping and snarling. They came to heel with their little headlights glaring like radiant eyes. One of the little motorcars snapped at Kay and almost got him.

From far away Kay heard something give way at the intake of the water. The rush of the flood-water increased suddenly threefold.

"Mr Hawlings," Kay said, "Mr Hawlings."

"Ah, is that you, Master Harker?" Cole said, leaning towards the bars of his cage. "If I were you, I wouldn't keep that size, Master Harker."

"Mr Hawlings," Kay said, "I have lost your Box and now I can't get back to my proper size, and the water's roaring in and he's got you all chained up here in these caves."

"I told you, Master Harker," Cole said, "that the Wolves were coming very close, and now they are here."

"Could you suggest something, Mr Cole, please," Kay said, "that I could do to help?"

"Do you remember the time when the Wolves came very close at Seekings yet I got away?"

"I do indeed," Kay said. "Could you do something of that sort now?"

"Why, I am not so sure, Master Kay," Cole said. "Have you such a thing as a pencil and a bit of paper?"

"No, I have not," Kay said.

"That's a pity," Cole answered, "but if you'd come up into my cell here through the bars . . . Now, you see in the corner there my coat that they took from me. I can't reach it, I am chained. If you can rummage in the pockets you should find a bit of paper and a pencil."

Sticking from one of Cole's pockets was a piece of timber, which looked like a newly-cut larch sapling. Near it was a pocket-book some four times bigger than Kay himself.

"I can't use these," Kay said.

"Get down into the pocket, Master Harker," Cole said, "for inside, if you grope, you may find a bit of lead that was broken off and a crumpled sheet or two."

Kay crept into the pocket, which was rather like going into a coal-mine. There were some crumbs like lumps of rock, but further down he found a piece of lead, in weight and shape like a poker. Near it was a piece of folded paper. He dragged these out into the light.

"I have got them," he said.

"Good," Cole said. "Now, are you a good hand at drawing?"

"No, I'm not very good," Kay said, "except at horses going from right to left."

"Well, suppose you draw horses," Cole said, "coming to bite these chains in two."

Kay opened the folded sheet of paper and bent back the crumpled corners, suddenly aware that the Wolves were Running with a little whirring snarl. Little motorcars with wolf-heads rushed from different points of the cave and snapped at him.

"Don't heed those, Master Kay," Cole Hawlings said.

It was not so easy not to heed them, for any of their bonnets was big and strong enough to snap him down into the engines, where he would have been champed up in no time.

"Hit them with the pencil, Master Kay," Cole Hawlings said.

"I don't think I can lift the pencil," Kay said, "it's too heavy."

"Well, try now," Cole said.

Kay tried and to his great delight found that he could lift this great fir tree of a pencil. As the motorcar came at him once more he smote the bonnet a lusty blow. The car at once upset and rolled over and over and over and the other little Wolf motorcars drew to one side and clashed their bonnets at Kay, snap, snap.

"Now draw, Master Harker," Cole Hawlings said, "two horses coming to bite the chains in two."

Kay went at it with the piece of lead like a poker, on the crumpled paper big as a blanket, which kept rolling up and hitting him. Sometimes, in earlier days, when he had drawn horses, he had felt that his effort had some merit. Somehow it seemed to him that what he drew was (for once) rather like a horse, but suddenly out of the air with a whirring yap came little aeroplanes with heads like wolves, snapping their propellers at him and trying to knock the lead from his hand.

"Bat them with the pencil, Master Harker," Cole said.

Kay lifted the lead with which he was drawing and smote one of the aeroplanes. The propeller snapped, the aeroplane crashed into two others, which spun round and round in flames and set fire to one of the motorcars, which exploded.

"That's the way, Master Harker," Cole said. "Now the other horse." The Wolves stood aside while Kay finished the second horse. Somehow they did look more like horses than cows; they hadn't got the Newfoundland-dog look that some of his horses had. In fact, the drawings did stand out from the paper rather strangely. The light was concentrated on them; as he looked at them, he saw that the light was partly fire from their eyes and manes, partly sparks from their hooves.

"They're real horses," he cried, "look!"

They were two terrible white horses with flaming mouths, striking great jags of rock from the floor, and in an instant, there they were, one on each side of Cole Hawlings, champing the chains as though they were grass, crushing the shackles, biting through the manacles and plucking the iron bars as though they were shoots of a plant.

"Steady there, boys," Cole said to the horses, as he rose and stretched himself.

He put on his coat, pocketed the paper, pencil and lead and placed Kay on one of the horses.

There before them the water was coming in, angry little eddies spun away with dead leaves and bits of twig; everywhere in that expanse of caverns there was the booming, roaring drumming of water echoes. The horses shied at the water. When their hoofs touched the stream they hissed and smoked, as white-hot metal will when wetted.

"Back a little, Master Harker," the old man said. "These horses are fiery. They can't abide water which puts out fire, as you know. We must proceed once more as before," he said, "with this paper and pencil. Draw me a long, roomy boat with a man in her, sculling her."

"I'm not very good at boats and I've never drawn a man sculling," Kay said.

"Draw now," Cole Hawlings said, "and put a man in the

boat's bow and draw him with a bunch of keys in his hand."

"Well, here's the boat," Kay said, "and here's the man sculling. Now, this is the man standing in the bow with a bunch of keys."

"Won't you give him a nose?" Cole said. "Men do generally have them and they're fine things to follow on a dark night when you can't see your way."

"I'm afraid the nose is rather like a stick," Kay said.

The old man took the drawing to the water, set it afloat and watched it drifting away. Somewhere far away to the left there came the noise of another rock or barrier collapsing under the pressure of the stream. The swirling of the water intensified and took to itself an angrier note. Bigger waves rushed out of the darkness at them and licked up more of the floor.

"The sluice-mouth has given way," Kay said.

"That is so," Cole Hawlings answered, "but the boat is coming too, you see."

Indeed, down the stream in the darkness of the corridor, a boat was coming. She had a light in her bows, somebody far aft in her was heaving at a scull which ground in the rowlocks. A man stood in the bows with something gleaming in his hand which looked like a bunch of keys. As he drew nearer Kay saw that this man was a very queer-looking fellow with a nose like a piece of bent stick.

Cole lifted Kay into a safe place in the stern-sheets and then turned to fetch on board the horses, who stamped, snorted and backed, not liking the water.

"And now, perhaps," old Cole said, "we'd better shove off to see if we can save some other prisoners. We haven't too much time, the way the water's coming in."

Kay looked along the corridor in the direction from which the water was pouring and saw something shining on the floor just above the edge of the stream. As it caught the light and sparkled, "Oh," Kay said, "look, look! It is your Box! The foxy-faced man must have dropped it."

"That is what it is," old Cole said. "And what quick eyes, Master Harker."

The old man went swiftly along the boat's length and vaulted over the gunwale into the stream, which was now over his ankles, caught the glittering treasure as it sailed by and vaulted back into the boat.

"Shove off," he said, and reaching to Kay he restored his shape at a touch. "That's rather better, Master Kay," he said.

"Indeed it is," Kay said, "and look, there are some oars floating by; they must have come from the lake."

He leaned over the side of the boat and salved one oar. Cole salved a second.

"Now, here we are," Cole said. "You stand on that side and shove her off the rocks and I will do the same on this side."

The current drove the boat into the alleys of blackness. The gallery in which they were floating was now almost full: they had to stoop to avoid the roof, often snapping off stalactites as they passed. As they entered another gallery, there, clinging to a stalactite, submerged up to the waist, was a drenched and sodden Rat, crying, "Pity a poor drowning man, an old naval pensioner what gave his youth for the Empire."

The man with the boat-hook said, "I'll fetch that chap a clip as we pass."

"No, no," Kay said, "he will help us to find the prisoners."

Cole Hawlings leaned over and pulled the Rat on board by his mangy collar. He was very cold, shivering with wet and terror.

"That's what comes," he said, with chattering teeth, "of having cisterns what burst. Time was when a cellar was a cellar, but now in these upside-downside days, folk keep their water with their wine, it seems."

"You know these cellars," Kay said, "where are the prisons with the clergymen in them?"

"Would they be what you call 'religious parties'?" the Rat asked. "They're along here, quite close. I was having as nice a

[151]

bit of religious biscuit as ever I ate, out of one of their pockets, when this water came in and I had to leave it. Such is life. That's what."

"They were along here?" Kay asked, pointing into the cave.

"They were along there," the Rat said, "as was the biscuit, but the biscuit will be pulp by this and the religious parties not much better. I suppose you ain't got a bit of bacon-rind you could give a poor man?"

"No, we haven't," Kay said.

"There's nobody keeps bacon-rind now," the Rat said. "They're too proud. Stuck up, I call it. Yah."

The boat drove under a low-hanging stretch of cave. There, near a stalactite, was a hole in the roof where Kay thought he saw the evil mouth of Alf, saying, "Hop it, Uncle!" As the boat drove under the stalactite Kay saw Alf stretching a dirty paw to the Rat, who sprang, caught it, swung himself to the hole and disappeared.

"Well, that's got rid of him," Kay said. "And there are the cells."

He was wrong: it was not the prison, it was the cell containing Caroline Louisa.

"It's all right," Kay cried, "we are coming to get you out."

"Try your keys, keyman," Cole said.

The man with the nose like a broken stick took his keys and opened the door without difficulty.

"I'm afraid you're sopping wet and half frozen," Kay said to Caroline Louisa as he helped her in, "but we'll soon get you to some dry and warm things."

At this moment they heard a hail from along the corridor: "Boat ahoy!" Somebody away there in the darkness of the alley was clapping hands and shouting, to attract attention.

"Who are you?" Cole cried.

"The Tatchester Cathedral staff," the Bishop's voice answered.

The boat drove on along the gallery. There, indeed, ankle-deep in the stream at the edge of the corridor, were the Bishop, the Dean, the Archdeacon, the Bishop's Chaplain, the Canons, the Minor Canons, the Precentor, the Organist, the Master Vesturer, the Bursar, the Librarian, the Chief Theologian – and Peter Jones. Cole and his crew helped them on board.

"How on earth did you all get out?" Kay asked.

"Oh," the Bishop said, "we've been out some time. A man and a woman came down to let out a friend of theirs called Joe. They went away with him, but after a minute Joe ran back with the keys and let us all out. We started off as he told us – the caves were lit at that time – but some terrible scoundrels, pirates evidently, wearing red aprons and sea-boots, came stamping along, led by one whom they called Rum-Chops. They said, 'It's no good going that way, all the lower caves are full already and our submarine's at the bottom of them, sunk.'

"They ran on and we followed them, but all the lights went out suddenly and we lost them. Since then we have been groping in the dark, almost at the end of our matches and our hope. Where are we, can you tell us?"

"Down in the heart of the Chester Hills," old Cole said, "but perhaps we'll get you out afore long. Give way, all."

"Where are the others?" Kay asked.

"What others?" the Dean asked.

"The Bell-ringers, the choirboys and at least half the choir," Kay said. "Oh and the Friends of the Cathedral and perhaps a lot of others."

"Shout, everybody," Cole said. "If they've not all been drowned they may hear us."

They shouted. Their voices echoed and boomed among the galleries and it seemed to Kay that some other sound of voices could be heard when the echoes died a little.

"Isn't that singing?" he said.

"What quick ears, Master Harker," Cole said. "Singing it is, away along there in the darkness. Heave all together now, for they must be sorely pressed."

They drove on against the stream until they heard the voices of the Bell-ringers and some of the choir singing 'Good King Wenceslas'. They shouted to reassure them and soon heard answering shouts. It was pitiful to hear the cries of the choirboys, saying, "Oh, if I'd only known, I'd never have cheeked my poor mother," or, "I wish I hadn't tied that tin can on the dog's tail."

"Cheer up," Cole shouted to them, "we'll soon get these locks open."

But to get these locks open was not easy. It was a different kind of lock from any the keyman had known; he tried one key after another.

"There's nothing for it," the keyman said solemnly, "but to compose yourselves unto a set of watery tombs."

"A set of watery rubbish," Cole said, heaving himself out of the boat to the door. "Why, no wonder you couldn't get them to work. The doors have spring catches, not locks at all . . . There you are. Lively with you now. That's the ticket. Are you all on board?"

"Yes," the Master Bell-ringer said. "This is the lot of us."

"We'll push off then, upstream," said Cole. "All lie on our backs and push the boat forward by our boots upon the ceiling."

The boat forged slowly ahead, with gurglings and cluckings of water. There was a great current against them and in some places the roof was very near. Kay could see little save archings of rock, which sometimes glistened with water and were sometimes hung with stalactites.

In one place the river ran through a wide cavern, the wall of which had been painted with a procession of men leading bulls and horses.

"That was our old religion, Master Harker," Cole said, nodding towards it. "It was nothing like so good as the new, of course, but it was good fun in its day, because it ended in a feast."

"You didn't eat horses," Kay said, "did you?"

"Ah, didn't we," Cole said.

After this they came into a narrow cave where the current was very strong. A sort of glimmer of light showed ahead. "There is moonlight and there is the sluice," Cole cried. Kay sat up.

There ahead was a silvery, shaking patch of light with a troubled roaring water pouring down in a fall. All about them the water eddied and jobbled. The boat tossed. The men, heaving with their boots, trebled their efforts and slowly it plunged forward against the rush.

"We will never get up a fall like that," the Bishop said.

"Where a salmon can go a man can go," said Cole. "This is only the first half, there is another fall above this. But lay hold of that tumbled tree there: it seems to me to be jammed firm. We can haul ourselves up by that."

Heaving all together they drove the boat into the rush and upward. Icy-cold water spurted all over them in a sheet, but they hove again, held all they had won and then hove onward to the top of the first fall.

There beyond them was another, shorter fall. In bright moonlight, at the mouth of this upper fall, Kay saw Abner heaving on a big winch handle which worked the sluice there. Abner was crying out:

"This thing has jammed. It ought to be wide but it's only half open. Open, will you!"

He hove and hove, then he left the winch-handle and dug at one of the cog-wheels with a knife.

"It's this cog that's jammed," he cried. "Open! Open!"

The boat forged forward to the foot of the second fall.

"We are in luck's way," Cole said. "See, there is an iron railing along the fall. We can heave up by that."

All hands seized the iron rail and drove the boat up. In the fury of his own effort, Abner heard nothing of the boat's approach. Kay saw him fling off his coat and again heave upon the winch. The boat was just behind him, but he knew nothing about her.

"Now," Cole said, "heave together – heave!"

Under their enormous heave the boat moved up in spouting, drenching jerks, drove on past the astonished Abner and the roaring fall, into the calm water of the lake.

Just as Kay passed Abner, something big swooped silently down and hovered just over their heads. Kay saw that it was one of the silent aeroplanes used by the gang. A light suddenly went up within its pilot house, by which Kay saw the Pouncer, the foxy-faced man and Joe leaning from the windows.

"Oh, Abner, did you really think to diddle me?" the Pouncer called.

"We've got all your jewels, Abner, ha-ha, what," the foxy-faced man cried.

"Goodbye, Abner," Joe called. Kay saw him lean further out and heave down what seemed like a bomb on Abner's head. It struck his head and exploded, but it was not a bomb, it was a two-pound bag of flour. "Got him!" Joe said.

Then the aeroplane lifted and was away into the air.

Blinded by flour, Abner came too near to the sluice, slipped, clutched, gave a startled cry and fell headlong into the torrent. For one instant Kay saw his legs, then they were sucked down into the gulf and disappeared. Before any of the people in the boat could fling off a coat and go in after him there came a swift warning noise of yielding in the structure of the sluice, now all sapped by the pouring of the cataract. It collapsed suddenly and utterly, the released water surged over it in one great swirl and filled its mouth as the boat drove out into the moonlit lake.

How the scene had changed since Kay had been there in the morning! The world was white with deep snow, many trees branchless or broken and those which remained bowed with great clots of snow upon them.

But what was happening at the Training College? There

were lights in all the windows, men floundering with lanterns outside the house, men calling. There were shouts of, "Here's another of them, hiding in the outhouse!" "Another pair of handcuffs for this chap, quick!" A party of men in the snow near the lakeside hailed to the boat to stop. The voice of the Inspector cried:

"Halt there, in the boat. Halt there! We have got you covered. Who are you?"

"The Bishop of Tatchester and all the prisoners," the Bishop called.

"Why, is that you, Your Grace?" cried the Inspector. "Pass the word there that the Bishop's saved . . . And you, Your Grace, would you ask your boatmen to come in towards the shore a bit." As the boat drew in he said, "Well, thankful I am to see you safe and sound again. Is this all your party?"

"Yes, everyone, we are all here," the voices answered.

"Pass the word to the wireless-men," the Inspector called, "to report All Saved. We are in time, it seems, but it was a near thing. I'll tell Your Grace how it came about."

"The Chief Constable thought we'd better act on Master Harker's information, but by that time the snow made it difficult to get here. However, what with planes and a will, we just did it.

"We have got most of these birds already and we'll have the rest before dawn – they can't get far in this snow – and we'll have the leader, too, for all he's so clever."

"He's gone down into the caves with the flood," Cole Hawlings answered. "I don't think any man will find any part of him again. Now, can we come ashore there?"

"No, don't you try it here," the Inspector cried, "you will never get through the snow on this side. By the way, have you got Master Kay Harker among you?"

"Yes," Kay cried, "I am here."

"Oh, I'm so glad to see you safe, Master Harker. It's through you that all the rest are safe," the Inspector called back. "Oh, and Master Harker, my nephew's down for Christmas and he has brought a pair of Belgian hares for you, as pretty a prize pair as ever I did see. Now, I must go to my men, but if you will shove your boat over there by that little bathing box, I think you will get ashore there without being sunk in the snow."

They gave way as well as they could with their two oars, a plank and a boat-hook. Presently, they ran the boat alongside the springboard and clambered out. The two horses whinnied and shook their manes, the two boatmen leaped on their backs and galloped away, straight up the slope of the Roman Camp. They disappeared over the rampart and were seen no more.

Indeed, now that the party had landed on the lakeside, they were amazed at the snow that had fallen in such a short time. Quite close to them, in what had been thickets in the wood, the wind had driven the snow capriciously into drifts that might well have been eight or nine feet deep. Kay, who remembered the path near the water, was amazed to see it so deeply covered.

But whatever the storm had been, it had now passed over, leaving a clear sky with a full moon shining so brightly that only the very big stars could be seen.

"It's eleven o'clock at night – after eleven," the Bishop said. "We'd better push on to Hope-under-Chesters and telephone from there."

They took a few steps along the path and then realised it might well take them all night to flounder through the drifts.

"Well, it's very disappointing," the Bishop said. "I'm afraid that after all there's no chance of our holding our Midnight Service in any church in the Diocese."

"Ah, I'm not so sure, Your Grace," Cole Hawlings said. "A travelling man who goes up and down the world, he finds ways of doing things – or doesn't he?" he asked Kay.

"I think he does," Kay said.

"Ah, you think he does?" Cole Hawlings said. "I think by this and that, we needn't give up hope yet. Listen, all."

The night was so still that standing there in the snow they

could hear the bells of nine churches ringing for Christmas. Above the noise of the bells Kay heard the jangling of lesser bells, or so it seemed. As it died away he felt he was mistaken, but immediately it broke out again, louder than before. They were bells not ringing to any tune or time.

"They're sleigh-bells," he said.

"Why, it's Father Christmas," said the Precentor, "coming with his team of reindeer."

But it was not Father Christmas. As the bells rang loud and clear, some lights appeared over the wall of the Roman Camp. Loping towards them, seeming hardly to brush the snow with their paws, came a magnificent team of harnessed lions drawing a long sledge driven by a lady whose eyes shone like sparks of fire. Kay saw at once that she was the Lady of the Oak Tree, who had stood by Bob's shop waiting for a word from Cole Hawlings. Outside the glove of her left hand was the strange ring with the St. Andrew's Cross upon it. Kay was amazed at the beauty and strength of the lions, their gleaming eyes and the way in which they tossed back their manes and snarled, or scuffled the snow with their pads, or showed their teeth with coughing, terrifying roars. He had never seen lions so beautiful, so powerful, nor with eyes so full of yellow flame.

"Get in, Bishop," the Lady said. "I can take half of you in this sleigh."

The Bishop and some of the others got into the sleigh, which seemed to be made of bright gold. It was heaped with great scarlet rugs and the furs of strange beasts. As soon as they were snugly in the sleigh under the rugs, the Lady called:

"I must leave before my team starts quarrelling with the other team."

She called to the lions, who bounded forward roaring. Kay saw them whirl round in a half circle, sending a great sheet of snow aloft, then they strode into the night, striking sparkles out of the air.

Kay had been delighted by the first sleigh, though the lions had a little scared him, but what was his delight when he saw that the second sleigh was drawn by unicorns!

"Oh," he said, "unicorns! And they always told me that they never existed."

But there was no doubt about these. It was a team of eight of the most beautiful unicorns that ever stepped, in build something like the very best white Arab stallions, only slimmer in the barrel and even neater in the leg. From their brows sprouted the most exquisite white horns about two feet long, sharp as needles and glowing like mother-of-pearl. Their traces and harness were of silver all studded with moonstones. They were driven by a man whose sleeves were hung with little silver chains and whose helm bore antlers; over his glove a red cross glowed upon a ring.

"Oh, it is Herne again," Kay said. "I do love going with Herne the Hunter."

"Jump in, the rest of you," Herne cried. "There will be room for all of you."

The sleigh was heaped with polar bearskins and great white fleeces from some mountain sheep. They all clambered on board and snuggled down into the fur. The driver called to his unicorns, who whinnied together and tossed up the snow with their hoofs before whirling round and away.

Cole Hawlings, who had a most beautiful voice, Kay thought, began to sing this carol:

> George took his lantern from the nail
>   And lit it at the fire-a;
> He said, 'The snow does so assail,
>   I'll shut the cows in byre-a.'
>
> Amid the snow, by byre-door,
>   A man and woman lay-a;
> George pitied them, they were so poor,
>   And brought them to the hay-a.

And there within the manger-bars
    A little child new-born-a,
All bright below a cross of stars,
    And in his brow a thorn-a.

The oxen lowed to see their King,
    The happy donkey brayed-a,
The cocks and hens on perch did sing,
    And George knelt down and prayed-a.

And straight a knocking on the door,
    And torches burning red-a,
The two great Kings with Melchior,
    With robes and wine and bread-a.

And all the night time rolled away
    With angels dancing down-a;
Now praise we that dear Babe today
    That bears the Cross and Crown-a.

It was most beautiful to drive through heaven thus, the shining country spread out below them, starred by the lights in villages and towns and musical with bells ringing for Christmas. Sometimes big white and tawny owls came floating alongside the sleigh, so close that Kay could stretch out his hand and stroke them.

"I say," he said, "how beautifully your unicorns move."

"You see, Master Kay, they hate being beaten by the lions," Herne said.

Kay had some misgivings as to what would happen if they caught up with the lions; then he thought that the drivers would probably be able to stop any fatal battle.

"There is the land you know," Herne the Hunter said.

Leaning over the rail of the sleigh Kay saw Condicote brightly lit and heard a few notes from the famous Condicote bells. The unicorns were now going so fast that it was only a moment before he saw the pinnacled tower of Tatchester Cathedral, floodlit for the great night, and all the lights of Tatchester.

'Of course,' he thought, 'everybody in the city has lit a window as part of the celebration.'

The unicorns swerved suddenly, then swerved again in a great sweep, cutting in ahead of the team of lions, who roared with rage at being passed. Dipping down, both sleighs skimmed into the snow and galloped its feathery surface for Tatchester Gate. A delicate, faint noise of bells came to them from the Tatchester Parish Churches.

"Ah there, listen now," one of the Cathedral Bell-ringers said to Kay. "Christmas Eve, near midnight, and no bells ringing in the Cathedral, no, not one. I never thought to hear so unChristian a silence, never."

"There's nothing stamps a Christian town more than its bells," Cole Hawlings said. "And a wandering man gives heed to bells, for often in the dark night they will ring him home, who would otherwise be ate by wolves and that."

"I could weep," another Bell-ringer said, "that our great Bell, Old Truepenny, of 1427, isn't throwing his tongue. He did ring in King Henry from the French Wars, Old Truepenny."

"We might still be in time to start Old Truepenny," the Dean said. "It is still not a quarter to twelve and we are nearly there. The only questions are, 'Can we reach the Cathedral in all this snow?' and, 'Have these ruffians who kidnapped us stolen the bell-tower keys, or cut the bell-ropes?' "

"We shall soon know, sir," Cole said. "The snow is deep: it has been a sad storm. Wolves' Weather, as we used to say in King Harold's time."

Now that they were over the Common, nearing the Gate, Kay could see what desolation the storm had wrought. The telegraph posts were down, the brackets of telephone wires had been wrenched from buildings and two old elms uprooted. The snow had drifted so deep at the Gate and in the High Street that no one had trodden it nor tried to drive it. The way was white, unspecked snow, deserted under the lamps.

The sleighs turned up the narrow lane known as St. Margaret's Barbican; the snow scattered from their runners with a crisp, soft, slithering swish; it was so deep in that narrow lane that Kay could see into the lighted rooms on the first floors of the old houses. He saw old black beams, old men and women drinking to Christmas or stooped over children's stockings, as they filled them with toys, neat surprise packages and oranges.

As they sped out of St. Margaret's Lane into the Parvice, the Cathedral suddenly rose up in front of them with its enormous black bulk, its windows unlit, its tower transfigured with floodlight, its ledges, mouldings and carvings all topped with snow. A man held up a lantern to check the unicorns, coming slowly past the team to the sleigh with his lantern lifted so that he might see who was there. Kay noticed that he was dragging a spade from his left hand and wearing a rough, dark sackcloth overall, and that other men, clad like him, were shovelling snow from the North Door.

"Ah, pass in, brothers, to St. Michael's Door, we've cleared the way for ye," the man who held the lantern said.

He waved his light and Herne moved the unicorns up the path to the door, the shovellers standing aside as they passed and calling blessings on them. They were all little men, with faces which looked white and tense in that dark place.

'I believe their heads are all shaven,' Kay thought. "Are these the Monks?" he asked.

"These are the Monks of the Abbey, Master Harker," Cole Hawlings said, "for on such a Christmas Eve what one of them would keep away? They've all come for the glory of St. Michael's Abbey."

Whoever they were, Kay long remembered the thin, eager faces of the monks on both sides of the approach lit by the lantern.

There was someone inside the porch, working at the fuse-box, with a clutter of tools and one little inefficient electric torch.

"Mind, please," this man said. "You can pass in to the side."

"Ha," the Bishop said. "It is Winter the electrician. Can you give us the lights in the Cathedral?"

"Why, welcome back, my Lord Bishop," he said. "Welcome indeed. But as to the lights, I can't give you as much as one, no, not a light, Your Grace. Whether it's these fuses or something worse I can't at the moment say."

"Just a quarter of an hour," the Dean said, "to robe and get the bells and lights and organ going. I wonder, will that snow-shoveller very kindly lend me his lantern? Come then, to the Dean's Cell, where we shall know if all the keys have been taken."

He led the way into the end of the dark North Aisle, where he unlocked the office known as the Dean's Cell. He struck a light and lit the tapers which he sometimes used for heating sealing-wax. "No, they've left us alone," he said. "Here are all the keys."

There on the walls, neatly ticketed and hung with plaques of wood or brass to keep them from being easily pocketed, were all the Cathedral keys. Some clergymen in robes who had been waiting outside the office now welcomed him.

"I am Josiah Stalwart," one of them said. "We were all here ready to carry on in case of need. If you'll allow us, we'll go up to light the choir."

When they had gone the Dean gave his orders.

"Bell-ringers first," he said, "here are the keys of the Belfry. You may still have time to ring the bells in and start a chime before midnight. Now, where has my Lord Bishop gone?"

"He has gone to robe," the Bishop's Chaplain replied. "He promised long ago to bless the Bell-ringers in the Tower tonight before they begin to ring."

"I was afraid for a moment," the Dean said, "lest he should have been captured again. Now, Vergers, take quickly all the wax candles in the storeroom and set them in the old sconces in the Nave and in the Transepts where they will at least make the darkness visible. Choirboys, quick, to the Vestry to robe. Anyone who has nothing to do with the service get out candles, please, with the Vergers and help to light the doors: we must let in the people in a moment. Who are those there, please? Oh, Mr Hawlings and Kay, will you very kindly take these old bronze incense tripods to the West Doors, put wax candles in them and light them so that the people coming in may see where they are treading."

Kay had not see him enter the Church, but when he and Cole had placed the bronze tripods near the Great Entrance, lo, there was Arnold of Todi beside them, looking madder than ever, brighter in the eye and queerer in his way.

"Ha," he said. "This is Feast of Nativity? You will pardon and excuse, this night, he Christmas?"

"Yes, yes," Kay said. "Christmas *dans cinq minutes*."

"Ha," Arnold said, "then I'm back in Anno Domini?"

"Yes, to be sure," Cole said, "and you must have a sup from my bottle that I brought all the way from Spain for you. And here is your Box of Delights that you have been parted from for so long."

"No no," Arnold said, "keep it, keep it. Now that I'm back in Anno Domini I'll stay there, thank ye. But you must have here a sup from my bottle from a temple that Alexander took. See now, I will show."

He produced a small glass bottle which he opened over one of the bronze incense tripods. He poured into the cap of this a little fragrant oil from his bottle and a few drops more into the second of the censers. "Watch now," he said.

As Kay watched, the oil burst into a bright light which lit up that end of the Nave.

"So Alexander found it burning," Arnold said, "in that

[165]

temple beyond the Gedrosian Waste, or one of the other Wastes. It will burn for seven hundred years, being Oil of Eternity."

Kay heard the people outside the West Doors cheering, with cries of "Hurray, there go the lights! There's going to be a service after all." Some hands pounded on the doors as Kay and Cole turned the giant key in the lock and dragged back the bolts one by one. All Tatchester seemed to be gathered outside there, waiting to get in.

"Oh," some were saying, "whoever's going to take the service? Have they found the clergy?"

"No, indeed," others said, "nor ever will, I'm afraid." "No, the poor Bishop's in his grave by this." "I'm told the Dean's legs have been found done up in brown paper, gaiters and all, in the Brighton waiting-room. These people who go murdering are just like wolves, they stick at nothing."

As Cole Hawlings seized one leaf of the double door, they seized the other, swinging the great doors back as far as they would go. The light from the tripods lit up a sea of faces gathered there, cheering the opening of the doors.

As the cheers rose, Kay saw that a great table had been laid immediately outside the Door, heaped with boxes of chocolates, bottles of sweets, dolls of all sorts and sizes, bats, balls, hoops, peg-tops, humming-tops, boxes of bricks and of soldiers, toy ships, kites, toy aeroplanes, crackers, fruits, books, papers, musical instruments and charming little mechanical toys. By this table were the three Jones girls, each dressed in white, with the Dog Barney, who barked with joy to see Old Cole again.

"Walk up," Maria was saying, "walk up, Parents. This is the Jones' Christmas fund, organised by Maria Jones as a token of her gratitude for having been thrice expelled from school. Every parent of a child attending this service is entitled to one package per child."

"Hullo, Maria," Peter said.

"Hullo, you two. I hear they've got the scoundrels," Maria called. "We had it on the wireless, but we'll talk about that later . . . Is yours a girl or a boy, Madam?"

At this instant the organ sent out some spiring and quavering rumbles which passed into 'Sleepers, Wake'. Then, with a sudden burst of light, all the Cathedral lights went on, shone for one glorious instant, went out again, recovered and then burned clearly: the electrician had found out what was amiss.

Now that the West Doors were open, Kay could hear that the Cathedral bells were ringing. He stayed there listening to them for a moment or two, Old Cole beside him, saying, "A happy sight, a blessed sight, Master Harker, all these coming here to sing." Arnold of Todi went up the Nave to stare at the decorations, seemingly in a trance of pleasure at being back in Anno Domini.

"Just two minutes more to go, Master Harker," Old Cole said.

There came the sound of many men marching to a drum-tap. A clear voice called an order and with a clink of metal and grunt of leather the band of the famous Tatshire Regiment, the Tatshire Toms, moved into position inside the church.

Then Crash came the salute of cannon in the Barrack Square for the stroke of midnight. Organ and brass band struck up, full strength, the Vestry door curtains fell back to each side and out came the great Cathedral crosses and blessed banners with all the Cathedral choir and clergy, voices lifted aloft in 'O Come, all ye Faithful'. By this time the triforium and clerestories, as well as every space in the Cathedral, were packed with faces: all there sang as they had never sung, the singing shook the whole building.

Somehow it seemed to Kay that it was shaking the Cathedral to pieces – Kay himself was being shaken to pieces, his own head was surely coming off, still singing, through the Cathedral roof.

In fact, the Cathedral was not there, nor any of all that

glorious company. No, he was in a railway carriage on a bitterly cold day, the train was stopped, he was at Condicote Station with his pocket full of money, just home for the holidays and Caroline Louisa was waking him.

"Why, Kay," she was saying, "wake up, wake up. You have been sound asleep. Welcome home for the holidays! Have you had a nice dream?"

"Yes," he said, "I have."